Y0-BRE-912

MICHAEL and the SECRET WAR

MICHAEL and the SECRET WAR

Atheneum   1989   New York

For my mother and father

Copyright © 1985 by Cassandra Golds
First published in 1985 by Angus & Robertson Publishers, Sydney and London
All rights reserved. No part of this book may be reproduced
or transmitted in any form or by any means, electronic or
mechanical, including photocopying, recording, or by any
information storage and retrieval system, without permission
in writing from the publisher.

Atheneum
Macmillan Publishing Company
866 Third Avenue, New York, NY 10022
Collier Macmillan Canada, Inc.
First United States Edition 1989
Printed in the United States of America
Designed by Michael I. Kaye
10 9 8 7 6 5 4 3 2 1

Library of Congress Cataloging-in-Publication Data
Golds, Cassandra.
Michael and the secret war/Cassandra Golds.
—1st United States ed. p. cm.
Summary: Magical creatures from another world enlist the help of
Michael in a secret war.
ISBN 0–689–31507–4
[1. Fantasy.]   I. Title.
PZ7 G5699Mi   1989 [Fic]—dc19

"For now we see through a glass, darkly;
but then face to face: now I know in part;
but then I shall know even as also I am known."
I Corinthians 13:12

Contents

The Beginning

It all began at about four o'clock on a sopping Tuesday afternoon.

The rain, spearing down and bouncing back a little way, as if unwilling to stay, made the road a shiny black bar of licorice. The sea was the misty gray of smoke. The beach stretched out parallel with the road, divided from it by a low stone wall, a footpath, and a long line of dripping pine trees. Cars swished past on one side, the sea swished forward and back on the other, rain pelted recklessly from above. And along the path walked two boys.

They were both in school uniform—a sort of gray affair with a royal blue blazer—and both wore longish black raincoats. One, fair and practical and doing most of the talking, was holding their single black umbrella steady beneath the pelting flak of the rain. That was Paul.

But the other—dark, intense, with the large brown eyes of a fox, and getting wet because he wouldn't come in close enough for shelter—well, *that* was Michael Devine.

They must have walked about a third of the way, when it happened. Michael, renouncing the umbrella, stopped and walked quite suddenly to the edge of the embankment. Paul went on a few steps—then paused, uncertain.

"What're you doing?" he yelled above the rain. A car swished past and the sea answered unhurriedly. But Michael was silent.

"Look, come on, will you?" Paul yelled, peering through the haze of the rain. "You'll be *soaked.*" Michael, looking uncertainly out to sea, already was.

"Hmm?"

"I said, you'll be soaked. Come on, I can't wait all day— What the—?!"

For Michael, suddenly seated with his feet over the wall, was pulling off his shoes.

"What're you *doing?*"

"Taking off my shoes."

"But you can't just—"

"That's okay, you go on."

"What d'you mean, go on?" Paul shouted in exasperation through the rain. "I can't. You haven't got an umbrella...."

"So what's it to you?" said Michael, his eyes on the sea, peeling off his socks with a sort of triumph.

"Devine, you are the biggest bloody idiot! Look, will you come *on.* I'm not waiting—"

But Michael was busy shoving shoes and socks into his schoolbag. He left it there in the rain, jumped down onto the sand, and began to plod slowly toward the sea. Paul stood beneath his umbrella, frowning at Michael's back. Then he kicked at the nearest pine tree and went on home.

Michael was going to be alone rather a lot in the next couple of weeks. He was alone now, filled with a conviction that someone, somewhere, was trying to tell him something, and indifferent to the rain that dripped through his dark hair and down behind his shirt collar.

2

He had already forgotten Paul, and, with the smoky gray obscurity of the wet beach around him, he knew only that he must walk on. So he met the sea, stared out at it a moment while it lapped at his feet, and then began to walk along beside the waterline.

Then, as the storm began to slacken, there was a change—quite small at first—in the air. For the first time since he had begun to think something *should* happen, Michael began to think it *would*. The rain, lighter now, played with his hair, dripped off his nose. Gazing through the astringent haze, he paused for a moment.

Then he began to run.

Wet hair flopped on his forehead; his raincoat flapped out behind him. The waterlogged sand slipped, but Michael, straining forward with his head down, felt only that if he ran fast enough he might—just—be able to catch—to catch . . . But the rain dripped to a drizzle, and after a moment or two he slid to a stop. Washing over him was a sense of having run just a little too far, or too fast, or perhaps not far or fast enough. And, somehow, he had missed it.

He stood there, panting, baffled and frustrated, and swore to himself. Then, soaked, and his clothes beginning to chafe, he began slowly to retrace his steps. When suddenly, on the sand—

Letters. Three of them, about a meter high, scored on the wet sand and quickly collapsing as if recently cut:

S E I

Michael, staring at them as his heart thundered in his chest, didn't notice as his third-form German came to the helm. For it looked like part of a verb. But it sounded, as Michael repeated it to himself, over and over, on his wet way home, like *sigh*.

And that was how it began.

The Mirror Cracks

ome, for Michael, was a small block of flats, two stories and built in about the 1920s. All red brick and white windowsills, a matronly sort of place, it had been owned and kept up by his grandmother for a very long time. As Michael plodded up the last stretch of the hill, it seemed to loom, with maddening practicality, before him.

For it *could* have been his imagination. And even if he *had* seen them—those letters—well, so what? People were always writing things in the sand; there was nothing particularly strange about that. S E I, thought Michael, stepping over the gate, faintly conscious of the squelch of his shoes. "S E I," he murmured, standing, very wet, in the doorway, not wanting to go in. S E I.

The small vestibule, with its brown linoleum floor and its new orange rug, opened out, closed up before him. Michael leaned against the wall and gazed intently into space. No. 1 and No. 2, eyeing him with the impassive silence of all doors that shut off other people's flats, were unhelpful. But his grandmother, coming up the stairs from the laundry, was not the quiet type.

"Honestly!"

Michael started.

"Michael, you're dripping all over the floor! Take it *off*, for goodness' sake!"

Michael struggled obediently out of his coat.

"But you're *soaking*! Whatever have you been up to?"

"It's pouring," Michael protested a little lamely. "I—"

"You missed the bus, I suppose. Shoes off, too, please. I only did the floor this morning."

Michael, doing a partial strip in the vestibule, noted the wet-dog smell of his blazer.

"Now go downstairs and get changed—"

"Changed?"

"Michael, you are soaking wet! You'll be lucky if you don't catch your death as it is—"

"All right," said Michael.

Padding slowly downstairs, he was visited by a sudden impression of just what a wet dog looks like—all drips and despair. That's what he was: a dark-eyed dog, drenched.

"Sometimes I wonder about you," his grandmother said after him.

"So do I," said Michael, under his breath.

———

Michael lived in the cellar. But Juliet lived in the attic. It could only have been that way. The attic was a sort of haven, and Michael liked going up there. Changed, and climbing the ladderlike wooden stairs from the kitchen in No. 4, he called up:

"Hello, Jilly."

And Juliet, the eldest, eighteen, and rather beautiful, sat cross-legged at her desk in her beautiful room. Its green-leaved quilt and its latticed windows; its sloping roof and its potted plants; its walls covered like patchwork

6

with Jilly's drawings, all seemed to protect her, like a shell. Jilly herself, fair and blue-eyed, scribbled algebra with one hand and stroked the cover of a new book with the other. The gray cat sat at her elbow on the desk and eyed Michael insolently.

"Hi," said Jilly. "Look what I've got."

"*The Great Escape*," read Michael from the cover. "I've read that."

"You've *read* it?" His sister flicked through it, lovingly. "Why didn't you tell me?"

"You wouldn't've been interested then. Anyway, *The Dam Busters* is better, you know."

"*The Dam Busters*," said Jilly thoughtfully. "But that's not POW stuff, is it?"

"It is, almost. That's where they all came from, practically. The prisoners, I mean. When they were shot down—"

"Ach, so," said Jilly, who also did German. "I'd better write that down. Who wrote it?"

"Same bloke."

"All right." Jilly leaned forward, scribbled in the beautifully neat notebook where she kept information about her heroes, and sat back tickling the cat. "How was the test?" she said.

"Not too bad."

"Missed the bus, did you?"

"I—we—I had to walk—"

"Thought so. Golly, you're wet."

"Yes," said Michael, sighing, sitting on the bed. This beautiful room, he thought. I can't tell her.

"You do look depressed, Mike," said Jilly.

"I am, a bit," said Michael.

They eyed each other. Then Michael, as he noticed a

new sheet of art paper, said with interest, "What's that?"

"Oh," said Jilly, "I was going to show it to you. I thought you might like it."

"It's terrific," said Michael. "What is it?"

"It's an abstract."

"But you never do abstracts—"

Michael, staring at it, thought *SEI*, and sat up. For it was there, in the picture, a hint of something he had felt many times before. And especially that afternoon.

"What do *you* think it is?" he said sharply.

Jilly opened her math book.

"Oh, nothing, really, I suppose," she said in a busy voice.

But Michael wasn't listening. He had just found out what was wrong with Jilly's paintings—all of them. They were *too* nice; they seemed to ignore the bits she didn't want to paint. And this, this was a watered-down version of the beach that afternoon.

"Jilly . . ."

But there was a clatter on the stairs.

"Michael! Jilly!"

The youngest of them, Robyn—sandy-haired, small, freckled—burst into the cloistered calm of Jilly's chamber.

"I'm in it! I'm in it!"

———

It's an ill wind, Michael reflected, that doesn't blow anyone any good. The good news was that Susan Gibson had appendicitis. Bad for Susan, obviously, but good for Robyn because now *she* had the part. And it was the main part—the Princess. But she had only two weeks, and the lines would have to be learned quick-smart, Miss

8

Thom said, which would be all right, she would work *so* hard, but couldn't she borrow Michael's tape recorder, and, yes, she would be very careful.

But the tape recorder was in his room, in the cellar. And suddenly, Michael was afraid. For a moment he hardly understood what she was asking him.

"It's in my room," he said vaguely.

"Can I have it?" said Robyn.

"Well, yes, I suppose—"

"Where is it, then?"

"I'm not really sure—"

"Can I look?"

Michael started.

"No," he said hurriedly. "I'll get it."

And slid off the bed.

Down the narrow stairs from the attic. Through the kitchen. Out onto the landing. Down the stairs. Into the vestibule. Through the laundry. And down the final staircase, into the cellar.

At first, he was unsure. There seemed, indeed, to be nothing in particular to worry about, nothing unusual to be seen. There was the bed, with the Jilly-made bedspread. There were the posters, the record player, the desk, submerged in math assignments, album covers, paperbacks, and a half-written short story. There was his calendar hanging crooked on the wall. There was the window, looking out on the back garden, a little overgrown with creepers, and the old back door, stuck, and painted over. All quite normal. Except for the breeze, suddenly coming from nowhere, flapping the papers on his desk.

Michael scuttled instinctively to the window. But it was shut, as was the door. The wind continued to wheeze around him. And then his eyes slid to the dressing table. Frowning suddenly, he took a sharp step forward and peered into the mirror. For there was no reflection at all, only the wind rushing out at him—and a voice, in his head:

"*SEI, Michael. This is the Secret War. Will you let us in?*"

Michael, terribly alone, didn't even think.

"Yes," he said vehemently. "Yes, I will."

And the wind died suddenly, as if turned off at the point. Michael didn't actually see it happen. All he knew was that when next he looked, there was a single jagged crack, running like a knife wound through his reflection. And, through this, spilled the world of the Secret War.

Traffic with Angels

Michael screamed.

For what seemed like a long, long time afterward, he sat on the edge of his bed, just staring into the mirror. The room, except for the dull clink and patter of the rain in the drainpipes, was quite silent. Outside, rain dripped through the garden, and it was getting cool.

He barely heard the clatter of feet down the stairs, was barely conscious of two figures appearing suddenly in the doorway.

"Michael?"

Juliet, tall, prefectlike in her white blouse and green plaid school skirt, made a hesitant entrance. Robyn, little and curly, tumbled into the room, pushed past her, and peered into Michael's face.

"Michael," said Jilly again.

"You should've seen Mrs. Beasley, Michael!" said Robyn, who did nearly perfect imitations of everyone in the flats. "You should've seen her! *Bounding* up the stairs, she was, and I was coming the other way! Golly, what a *whack*! 'I wouldn't go down there, love, not if I were you,' she says. 'I'm afraid something dreadful—'"

"Robyn, stop it, she might hear," said Jilly. "Michael, what's wrong?"

Michael dragged his eyes from the mirror. Of course, he couldn't possibly explain. Jilly's face, anxious but not wanting him to tell her anything she didn't want to hear, stopped him. As for Robyn, she might have laughed, and he couldn't have stood that. All the same, a small persistent part of him wanted to air it, to be told it was just a touch of the sun or not enough vitamin C. He started to say something, changed his mind, and then pointed at the mirror.

His sisters gasped.

"Seven years' bad luck," said Robyn automatically, without conviction.

"How did it happen?" Jilly demanded. "Did you hurt yourself?"

Michael, struck by this new possibility, inspected himself briefly.

"I don't think so," he said huskily. "I—p'raps I—kicked it?"

It sounded weak.

"Well, I don't know," said Jilly lamely. "Can't you remember doing it?"

"N-not really—"

"She must've heard the glass breaking," said Jilly, referring to Mrs. Beasley. "But she said it was an awful racket—"

"I—I think I yelled, actually."

"*Yelled?*" Jilly searched his face. "Michael, you're awfully pale. You didn't pass out or anything, did you?"

Michael, suddenly weary, knew she was clutching at straws. "I might've, I s'pose," he said.

"Did you have any lunch today?" asked Jilly. "Oh, Michael, you didn't, did you?"

"Man does not live by bread alone," said Robyn brightly.

"The way Michael eats," said Jilly, "he's lucky to be alive at all." Then she smiled and put her hand on his arm. "You'd better come upstairs," she said, being Jilly-the-motherly. "You'd better have an aspirin or something."

And Mrs. Beasley of No. 2, plump and kindly, stood at the top of the stairs.

"Everything all right, then, love?" she said with a hesitant smile. "You had me worried, I can tell you."

"I—er—"

"He cracked his mirror," said Robyn importantly. And Jilly, with a cool hand on his shoulder, pushed him through the laundry. Michael had a vivid impression of being himself when much younger and was just registering this when he noticed Simon, the artist of No. 1, shrugging on a cardigan in the vestibule. He hesitated, gave Jilly the sort of look he often gave her, and said, "Everything okay?"

But Jilly just blushed to the roots of her golden hair and muttered, "Yes," before pushing Michael hurriedly up the stairs.

Once in the kitchen, however, it was all quite simple. Jilly heated milk, Michael sat morosely on the table, and Robyn sort of fluttered about. So the lecture began.

"You don't sleep, you don't eat, and you work too hard," Jilly said, stirring the milk. "No wonder you're a nervous wreck."

"I don't work too hard," said Michael, pouncing on the only thing he could possibly deny.

"Where's Bruce?" said Robyn.

"His name is Hamlet, thanks, Robyn, and I don't know. What d'you mean, you don't work too hard? You must be doing something at that desk of yours. It's covered with rubbish—"

"It is not," said Michael, who wrote failed masterpieces into the small hours of the night. "It's only—"

"But it's time for his Zap'em," said Robyn. "You said I could do it, this time."

"Well, if he's not here, he'll have to do without it."

Robyn was scandalized.

"Drongo can't get along without his Zap'em! He'll be *crawling*—"

"His name is *Hamlet*," Jilly snapped. "You're going to have to start eating properly, Michael—it's just common sense." She poured hot milk into a cup, mixed in a spoonful of honey, tore at the foil of the aspirins, and doled out two. "Now take those and for heaven's sake go to bed."

"At half-past five?" Michael protested.

"You're a hard woman, Jilly," said Robyn. "First you let Victor go without his Zap'em, and now you're sending Mike back down to face that stinking hovel—"

"Well, you could at least have a rest until teatime," Jilly amended. "You look positively ill."

"Oh, thanks," said Michael.

"*There* he is!" cried Robyn.

The cat, about to stroll in through the doorway, stopped dead and headed off back down the stairs. Robyn bolted after him. And Michael, sniffing distastefully at the cup, reflected that he hated milk.

Nevertheless, he decided to appease Jilly by lying for half an hour on the settee in the living room. He didn't sleep, but then, he rarely did. He couldn't have gone back downstairs—not for a while, anyway.

It was half-past six. Jilly, standing in the kitchen doorway with her hands clasped in front of her, eyed Michael with disapproval.

"Our neurotic budgie," said Michael, peering through the bars of the cage.

"No wonder he's neurotic," said Jilly, "with you staring at him like that."

"I can't help it," said Michael. "Look at the way he throws the seed around."

"He's probably trying to defend himself."

"Well, it's lucky he hasn't got anything *lethal* to throw."

"I suppose that's what he thinks about you, Michael."

Michael, defeated, bowed decorously in Jilly's direction. Then he said: "Listen, Jill. That painting of yours—"

When suddenly, the door opened, and in spilled Mrs. Devine and Robyn.

"—the Princess," Robyn was saying, "and Miss Thom said it was a jolly good thing I could read so well, because she would've been *stuck,* well and truly—"

"I hope this doesn't call for sewing," said Mrs. Devine. "I've got my hands full as it is, and Jilly's got her exams."

"We could look in the box," said Robyn hopefully. "There should be *something*."

Michael, feeling abruptly washed out, began to throw things around the table, his version of setting it.

"No need to be so rough," said Mrs. Devine. "*Michael!*"

"Sorry."

"But there should be something, shouldn't there?" Robyn persisted.

And Juliet, mashing potatoes in the kitchen, said fondly, "I used to have a sort of dress, a long one with a flounce, when I was about—"

"Where is it?" Robyn demanded.

SEI, thought Michael, for the sixtieth time.

"You might not like it," said Jilly cautiously.

"It might not fit you," said Mrs. Devine.

"Where is it?" said Robyn.

"Probably in the box somewhere," said Jilly, banging a spoon on the saucepan. "We'll go through it afterward, if you like."

Michael, looking for something to drink, found Jilly's math book in the fridge, rescued it, and thought uncomfortably about the mirror. "There's nothing to drink," he said aloud.

"I saw Mrs. Beasley downstairs," said Mrs. Devine.

"Oh, yes," said Jilly. "She was a bit worried this afternoon."

Michael coughed to himself, went in, and sat down at the table. Jilly followed, with a plateful of something he knew he couldn't manage.

"Have a glass of water," she suggested.

"You ought to see the crack," said Robyn. "Enormous, it is."

Mrs. Devine clicked her practical tongue. "Dear-oh-dear! Now we'll have to get you a new dressing table."

Michael thought that was the least of their worries.

"Yes," he said. "I'm sorry, Gran."

"Well, it's thirty years old, after all. And anyway, you can make do for the time being, can't you?"

"Yes, of course."

His grandmother studied him.

"I still don't see how you managed it."

"I think I must've kicked it," said Michael. "And it gave me a bit of a shock, so I yelled."

"Hmm," said Mrs. Devine.

16

Jilly flushed, glanced at Michael, and pushed a glass toward him. Robyn helped herself to bread and butter. And Michael, not hungry, stabbed at a pea.

"Oh, yes," said Jilly hurriedly, "I've been meaning to ask you, Gran. Is it all right if Sarah Jane comes over Thursday afternoon?"

"Who's Sarah Jane?" said Robyn.

"She's new," said Jilly, "and she's in second form, and I'm supposed to be looking after her. She wants me to coach her in French."

"*Coach?*" said Mrs. Devine.

"Yes, well, she's never done it before, you see. And everyone else's done a year. So she's quite behind—"

"Quite cluey of her," said Robyn acutely, "to pick on the scholarship kid."

"I don't think she could've known that," said Juliet, hurt. "It's just, I'm her class prefect, and—"

"What did you say her name was?"

"Sarah Jane Yardley."

"Well, it's all right by me. Don't wear yourself out, though, Jilly. You've got exams, remember."

"Can I look in the box now?" said Robyn.

And teatime dispersed over washing up and cat feeding. Unnoticed, Michael managed to slip most of his dinner into the kitchen bin. He was good at that sort of thing.

———

Michael, as you will have gathered by now, was the Devine family's resident insomniac. But that night, for once, there were two very good reasons for not sleeping. Firstly, there was the cracked mirror gaping down on him. And secondly, there was his troubled conviction that

17

something was going to happen. He was certain of this, so certain that it hardly seemed worth going to bed.

However, he had a shower, donned striped pajamas, and lay silent in the cool darkness of his room until about eleven. Then he got up, padded upstairs, and began to make a cheese sandwich.

Not only was Michael habitually unable to sleep, he had also discovered that he was only hungry in the middle of the night. And the only thing he ever wanted was a cheese sandwich. Usually, if he banged around a bit, Jilly would come down, tall and fair in her long, pale green bathrobe, and talk to him while he ate. But Michael could be very quiet, and tonight he was. He didn't want Jilly to come down.

Michael sat in the pitch-dark dining room and ate his cheese sandwich. When he went back into the kitchen, there was someone tapping on the window.

Michael opened it.

"Thank you," said the visitor. He climbed like a cat over the sink and sank onto the floor in his silent black shoes. "Could you draw the blinds, please?"

The voice was soft, polite, and accented so that it lingered on the consonants. Michael obliged.

"Is—is someone looking for you?"

"Someone is always looking for me. I am sorry, Devine, did I frighten you?"

"No—I—er—" Michael gestured lamely. "Do—do you always do that?"

The visitor, standing off a little in his black suit, white shirt, and black tie, gave a curious duck of his head and peered upward. It was a habit with him.

"Do what?"

But it was difficult to explain. It was just that he didn't

18

seem all there, from one moment to the next. Sometimes, as Michael watched, there was more of him than at others. One seemed constantly to be looking at him through a kaleidoscope. He seemed tremulous, as if never quite sure whether or not he should actually exist—or was it Michael who was never quite sure . . . ?

The visitor, with a quick glance around the kitchen, located the clock on the electric stove.

"Excuse me," he said.

He held his hand out toward the clock for a moment, palm upward. Then he flicked out his other arm and uncovered something on his wrist, which looked a bit like a watch. Only it was bright emerald green and seemed to shed sparks. He passed his palm over it quickly, then checked it.

"Good," he said. "Thank you."

He smiled a quick pink-and-white smile. His eyes, steely gray, blazed at Michael.

"Thank you," he said, "for letting us in."

"That's all right," said Michael, dazed.

"It won't be easy," warned the visitor. "It is never easy to be in two worlds at once. But for better, for worse, once you see it, you're in it. I'm glad you are on our side."

He paused and ran his fingers through the tufts of his jagged fair hair. He had the most pointed ears Michael had ever seen.

"I wish you only had to see the nice things," he continued, a little more carefully. "Because there're a lot of those, you know. But you can't see the nice without also seeing the nasty; that's the way it goes, Devine. Besides, we need your help. And we couldn't ask it if you weren't able to see our enemies—"

"Your enemies?"

19

"Yes," said the visitor. "*Them.* This is a mission, Devine. I have just begun it. It is They who will try to stop us."

"Then you're at war?"

"This is the Secret War, Devine. Few ever see it. But it's going on, all the same, everywhere, always: Now that you are a Helper, you will come to know that. But don't be too grateful to us for bringing you in. There's danger in helping us. They'll hurt you, Devine. They'll try to change you. They'll even try to make you think you're losing your mind."

"But how can *I* help *you?*" said Michael.

The visitor smiled his sudden smile, a little wryly.

"All you have to do, Devine, for now, is to shelter those of us who cross your path. My friends are often defenseless; if I tell them you are one of us, they will be able to come to you when in need. We will try not to make it too difficult for you, but—"

"Who *are* you?" Michael asked suddenly.

The visitor peered out carefully through a slit in the blind.

"Who am I?" he echoed. "Oh, I see. Just call me the Sparrow."

Then, for the first time, breezy, came the sound. "*SEI,* Devine," whispered the voice through the flutter and sigh of the Sparrow's departure. When Michael looked up, he was gone.

The Swanningwren

The cellar, cool and lonely in the bleak light of the early morning, was silent as Michael awoke. He was just beginning to think confusedly about broken glass when the door opened and a small, curly something looked in. Robyn.

"Michael?" she whispered.

Michael stirred, and Robyn, pale in a pink quilted bathrobe, pattered over to the bed. She bent over him and peered into his face.

"Michael!" she repeated urgently.

He flinched and squinted up at her.

"What's the time?"

"Doesn't matter. There's something on my bed."

Michael sighed, sat up, and yawned.

"There's what?" he said.

"Something yukky," said Robyn, "on my bed."

"On your *bed*? You've been dreaming, Rob."

"I haven't. It's *there*. I—"

"Oh, all right then." Michael crawled over the quilt, fished his bathrobe off the floor, shouldered his way into it, and disentangled the cord. "If I come and look, will you go back to bed?"

"You look first," said Robyn, "then come and get me."

Michael watched bleakly as she snuggled down.

"*Honestly,* Robyn—"

But there was nothing for it. Yawning. Michael went upstairs.

Hamlet the cat arched in the doorway of Robyn's room—his tail fluffed up like a bottlebrush. Michael stiffened, peered into the 5:30 grayness, and gasped.

For there was, indeed, something on Robyn's bed.

"Would—would you mind calling off your animal?" came the voice, tinkling, nervous. . . .

Michael kicked frustratedly at the cat. Suddenly, it was all coming back to him—the beach, the mirror, the Sparrow—everything. This, he supposed, was his first refugee.

"Bugger off, Hamlet," he said.

Offended, the cat eyed him with contempt and made a dignified exit.

Michael switched on the light.

"You—you are a friend?" came the lovely, bell-like voice from the bed.

Michael sank back into the corner of the room.

"You—you won't give me up?" the voice pursued.

"I—er—" Michael stammered.

"They told me to say *SEI.* They said you would understand."

Michael, leaning back against the wall, had to shut his eyes for a moment. For there, on the bed, revealed in the golden glow of the light, sat the most beautiful creature he had ever seen. It was black, sleek, and short-haired, the size of a very small cat; and its ears, pointed, were about a third of its body length. Its eyes were great and golden, and it had a tail that fanned out and upward, bushy like a fox's. But the snout was that of a cat, and the whiskers that twinkled delicately under the lamp were quite golden, adorning the black fur like rare jewelry. Michael blinked.

"You are a Helper, aren't you?"

"Er, yes," said Michael, "at least, I *think*—"

"And your name is Michael." The creature started suddenly and looked around the room. "You—you won't give me up, will you?" she said urgently.

"*No,*" said Michael.

And the creature sighed.

"Then you must help me. I am the Swanningwren, and I am in danger."

"The—the Swanningwren?" Michael repeated, dazed.

The creature inclined her beautiful head and lifted one paw, in a regal manner. The gesture was momentarily lost on Michael—then he saw what was expected of him. He crossed the room hurriedly, took the black paw in his hand, and set his lips on it. And the Swanningwren just gazed at him with her great golden eyes.

"You must protect me, Michael. I have no other hope. I *must* get across the border, but until they can break it for me, I'm trapped."

"Trapped?" said Michael. "Who's after you?"

"*Them.* But your friends, they are helping me. In the meantime I must wait. Their magic is strong; I shan't break through it alone."

"*Magic?*" said Michael.

For after all, who said anything about magic? Wasn't it a war he was in—?

But the Swanningwren just gazed at him.

"You may sit down," she said.

Michael, confused, was glad he had not already done so.

"Wh-what do you mean, across the border?" he asked carefully.

The Swanningwren glanced furtively around her.

"I am caught between two worlds," she whispered. "An accident. I do not belong here, and I cannot stay. If I do not get out within five hours, I will die. Your friends have promised to get me out—but others will do their utmost to prevent that. Do you understand?"

"I think so," said Michael.

The Swanningwren glanced again around the room.

"Well," she said nervously, "that is all you may know. I am safe, beneath your shelter, but if I am trapped here for too long . . ."

Michael saw tears fill her great, golden eyes.

"Oh," he said, distressed. "Please don't . . ."

But there was nothing he could do. He said instead: "Look, can't I get you anything?"

The Swanningwren blinked her dewy eyes.

"I—I'm not sure if I eat what is in your world," she said huskily.

"Do you drink at all?" Michael said, groping in the dark. "Milk, perhaps?"

But the Swanningwren inclined her beautiful head.

"Bring me whatever you have," she said humbly. "And I'll see what I can do."

Michael needed the excuse to get away for a moment. Her presence was somewhat overwhelming. He darted into the kitchen. Passing the cabinet where his grandmother kept her fine glasses and china, he caught sight of the cut-glass decanter with the amber liquid in it, which they never touched. It occurred to him for that reason that it was probably the best thing they had in the house. So he took out one of the prettiest saucers, grabbed the decanter, and lugged them into Robyn's room.

The Swanningwren started when he came back in, then looked away apologetically.

"I'm sorry," she said. "I'm feeling a little nervous, I think."

Michael, standing in the doorway, began to say something, then, embarrassed, changed his mind. He wasn't even beginning to get used to her. He glanced about him, then plucked a cushion off the floor, laid it on the bed, and put the saucer on it. He filled the saucer with the golden drink, stood back, and coughed.

"Er—d'you think you might—"

"Thank you," she said graciously, and began like a cat to lap it up.

It had a certain effect on her. She looked up brightly, and her eyes twinkled. "That was very nice," she said.

Michael felt like throwing a party.

"W-would you like some more?"

"Oh, no," said the Swanningwren coyly. "That will suffice, thank you."

Michael grinned shyly at her, took the saucer and the decanter, and headed for the kitchen. With exquisite timing his grandmother appeared.

"You're up early, Michael."

"Yes— I —er—"

"Michael, don't go to school, today, dear—you're not looking at all well. We might pop up to the doctor, I think."

"Oh—yes—well . . ."

"Since you're up, though, you might like to take

Simon's breakfast down—I've got some nice stew there for him."

"Yes—I—of course . . ."

"That's a good boy. It's on the table. Will you wake up Robyn for me?"

And she was gone, slippering down the hall. Michael looked at the decanter, looked at the saucer, and heaved an immense sigh of relief.

———

But it was going to be a problem—he could see that. After all, he could hardly leave her alone—and he wasn't keen to take her visiting, either. Unless . . .

"Are you sure you don't mind?" he asked again, trying to get her comfortable. She was clinging, like a bat, to the front of his pajama shirt, and it wasn't exactly bliss for Michael, either.

"I'll be all right," she said, muffled beneath his bathrobe. "Can you see me?"

Michael looked critically into Robyn's mirror. It was lucky, he reflected, that the Swanningwren was so slender. When he bunched up the bathrobe, the lump hardly showed—and perhaps if you weren't looking for it . . .

"Anyway," he whispered as they went downstairs, "we really haven't much choice."

And they hadn't. The main thing, thought Michael, was to be natural. So all he had to do was . . .

Simon's door was ajar.

"Hello?" called Michael into the flat.

"Come in, Michael," came a faintly distracted reply.

It was hardly past 6:00, but practically no hour was too early for Simon Collins. He was only a part-time artist, because he couldn't make a living out of it, and so he painted from five to nine every morning before getting on with the multitude of odd jobs he had fixed up for himself all over town. Michael didn't see all that much of him, but he liked him a little better every time he did. He was to like Simon very much indeed before the fortnight was out.

But that was in the future. Michael, concentrating on being normal, came through the hall and out into Simon's verandah, with its latticed windows, and its canvases, and its strong and pleasant smell of turpentine. He patted nervous reassurance to the beautiful thing on his chest, his hand inside his bathrobe like Napoleon, and said, "Hi."

Simon, glancing up, rubbed his nose and left a smear of red paint there.

"Hello, Michael," he said, with one of his very rare smiles.

"Gran sent this down for breakfast," Michael said. "It's some sort of muck, and you've got to heat it up, so d'you want me to put it on the stove for you?"

"It's in a saucepan, is it?"

"Yep."

"All right then."

That, translated from Simon-language, meant: Thank your gran for me, thanks for bringing it down, and it's nice to see you, Michael.

Well, thought Michael, beginning to relax, this is going all right. The Swanningwren, apparently, didn't agree. She slipped, hissed, and accidentally gripped his flesh.

"*Ouch!*"

"Hmm?"

"Er—nothing." Michael, wriggling, thought: *Change the subject, stupid!* "What're you doing?" he said quickly.

"Who, me?" said Simon. "Painting. Why?"

Michael, getting her settled again, switched the hot plate onto "very high" (for he did nothing by halves) and clanged the saucepan onto it.

"I meant, what're you painting?" he said.

Simon frowned at him. This did not appear to mean anything in particular; it was just his habitual expression. "You can have a look, if you like," he said. And stood back, jealously studying his work with keen blue eyes.

Michael walked over to the painting, holding carefully onto his bathrobe.

"I like it," he said, after a moment. "What is it?"

"Sleeping Beauty. I want to show it to someone; it might get me a job."

"What, illustrating?"

"I hope so. You never know . . ."

But Michael was thinking. He was dimly aware of a certain something in Simon's style. His work seemed more truthful than Jilly's. Jilly's paintings were beautiful, but somehow insipid, whereas his were beautiful and *hard*. Then Michael had it. Just as Jilly left things out, Simon seemed to leave too many in. But then, looking at the Sleeping Beauty, Michael thought he saw something familiar.

For a moment, the War fled his mind.

"Simon," he said hesitantly, pointing at the face. "That's Jilly, isn't it?"

Simon winced and frowned deeply.

"Damn," he said.

Michael, suddenly too embarrassed to stay, went into

the kitchen just in time to save the stew. He took it off the hot plate, and the froth subsided.

"It's ready," he called as casually as he could.

Simon came into the doorway, hands in the pockets of his jeans, and they looked at each other for a moment. Michael, turning back to the stove, was left with a vivid impression of wavy brown hair, bushy eyebrows, a nose straight and pointed like the letter V, and thin, hard lips. It was the face of some odd little animal, pointed and piercing, and the remarkably blue eyes reminded him of a trapped creature looking through the bars of its cage.

"I didn't *put* her in," he said, after a moment. "She just—sort of—turned up . . ."

"Yes," said Michael.

Simon hesitated. "Listen," he said, after a moment. "What *is* that you have in your bathrobe?"

"Yes, well," said Michael, "must be getting back upstairs, you know. Gran'll wonder where I've got to—and I—er . . ."

But just then, of all times, something occurred to him. Simon, he recalled, had done something at university about magic—and Michael, suddenly too alone, wanted advice. Could he perhaps . . . ?

And Simon stood gazing at him, a sad expression on his face.

"I—er—I can't tell you," said Michael, at length. "But, listen—you know quite a lot about—er—fairy tales, don't you?"

Simon frowned at him.

"I wrote my thesis on them," he said calmly.

"Well, I was wondering," said Michael quickly, "if you'd ever read about something being stuck between two worlds, sort of—*ow*!"

"Michael, are you in pain?"

"Yes. I mean, no. You know, when things get sort of—enchanted?"

Michael was getting a bit desperate. But Simon, looking away, just said, "Yes."

"I mean," Michael resumed, "when witches and things use magic to stop people, to make people . . ."

"Yes, I know what you mean," said Simon.

"Well, how d'you—I mean, they—er—fight against it?"

Simon looked for a moment as if he wished Michael would tell him exactly what this was all about. He started to say something, paused, then gave another of his rare smiles, and said: "If it's an enchantment, usually someone has to make a sacrifice. Like in *The Seven Swans*— all that nettle weaving. You remember that one, don't you? And then, of course, in *Sleeping Beauty*, the Prince has to fight through the enchanted forest to get to the Princess. It's the kiss that actually breaks the spell there, of course," he added, looking away quite suddenly.

Michael was visited by a sudden vision of Jilly, asleep, way up in the attic.

"Thanks," he said, abruptly, wanting only to get out. "That's a help." He smiled with embarrassment, went out through the little hall, and then heard the squeak of Simon's white sneakers behind him. Michael battled with shyness and finally paused in the doorway. It seemed only fair to say it.

"She's exactly right," he murmured, "for Sleeping Beauty."

Simon frowned.

"You won't tell her," he said, "will you?"

" 'Course not," said Michael.

And Simon, looking quite seriously at him, said, "You

know, Michael, you really shouldn't keep things in your
bathrobe like that. It could be dangerous."

Michael, biting his lip, went downstairs to wake
Robyn.

———

"All right," said Michael, leaning in the doorway. "*Out.*"

Robyn, very warm and ruffled, rolled over.

"Hmm?"

"Time to get up, Sunshine. Gran said."

Robyn, grumbling, sat up slowly.

"Did you put it out?"

"Put what—oh, *that.* Er—yes, I did."

"*Told* you." She slid reluctantly out of bed. "It's a big
crack, isn't it?" she said, glancing at the mirror.

"Yes. Hurry up."

"I'm *going.*" But she paused, yawning, in the doorway.
"Gee, your bathrobe looks funny, Michael."

"Look, pop off now, all right?"

Robyn, with a wounded look, padded upstairs.

Michael, sighing, shut the door, tore open his bathrobe, and placed his burden on the rumpled bed.

"Your *claws!*" he said.

"Sorry. But I don't see why you had to ask *him.*"

"Oh, he's reliable," said Michael. "Believe me, he's
reliable."

"All the same . . ." said the Swanningwren. And she
sat down, swaying a little.

"Are you all right?" said Michael quickly.

"Just—let me get my breath," she gasped.

Michael, worried, studied her.

"It's the air," she explained, at last. "One can't seem—
to get a breath . . ."

"But you—you've got five hours, haven't you?"

"You forget—I've already been here for two at least."

Michael felt himself lose color.

"*Oh.*"

The Swanningwren gazed at him with her great golden eyes.

"Why did you ask him, anyway?" she said.

Michael bit his lip and squinted at her. "Well," he said, "I was wondering, about me being a Helper. Maybe I'm supposed to *do* something."

"About getting me out?" panted the Swanningwren. "I don't think so, my dear. I don't think you could. The magic—you've no idea . . ." She closed her eyes.

"Yes," said Michael, "but anyone can sacrifice something, if they care enough. You don't have to be very magical to do that."

The Swanningwren started and looked up at him excitedly.

"I—I've just thought," she wheezed. "I—I wonder if—" but she was shaken suddenly by long, dry coughs. She closed her eyes again and tears squeezed from beneath the lids.

Michael put his hand on her beautiful head, his awe of her forgotten in an overwhelming wave of pity and frustration. "Oh, look," he said recklessly, "I'd do anything to get you out of this. Anything. If only I knew what—"

And then, something happened. Later, Michael could never explain it properly—although, at the time, it seemed quite easy to understand. But it was a feeling, more than anything—a feeling of having somehow, briefly, crossed over into another way of looking at things. And the air, for Michael, seemed to shift—

"Oh!" cried the Swanningwren. "Michael, I was right! It was your *wanting* that did it! Michael, I'm free, I can cross . . ."

She sprang up, peered at something a little way in front of her, careered into midair, and was gone. Amazed, Michael looked around. After a moment, he heard:

"Thank you, Michael, darling!"

The tinkling voice faded.

Michael sat down heavily on the crumpled bed. Then, his eyes fell on the mirror.

Rigid, he watched the red streaks swoop across the crack, making letters—words—running, puddling, disappearing as he read:

YOU HAVE ALREADY HELPED TOO MUCH.

The Room That Wasn't There

The doctor's waiting room, painted pale blue and equipped with the obligatory tabletop full of magazines, smelled of floor polish and patients. Michael stared out at the main street, sank further into his chair, and wondered about the Swanningwren.

"Mrs. Devine and Michael?" said the receptionist pleasantly, card in hand. "Doctor will see you now."

Michael trailed his grandmother into the office.

The doctor eyed him, speculatively.

"Off his food, eh?"

"He says he can't sleep," Mrs. Devine supplied. "And I'm afraid we just can't get him to eat properly. He's not been well for a good few weeks."

"Hmm," said the doctor.

Michael avoided his eyes.

"Any dizzy spells, headaches?"

"No."

The doctor leaned forward.

"Anything worrying you, Michael?"

You bet!

"Oh, no . . ."

"You seem a bit nervous, all the same. It could be just tension. Exams coming up, I suppose?"

34

"In three weeks."

The doctor nodded.

"Well," he said, "I wouldn't worry, if I were you, Mrs. Devine. He hasn't enough symptoms for it to be something serious. And you know the sort of pressure on kids today. It's enough to turn anyone off his food. Ever miss your parents, Michael?"

The abruptness of the inquiry caught him by surprise.

"That was five *years* ago—" he stammered.

"Yes, I know. Only, you're at the stage to start analyzing it now. Never mind. I'll tell you what. We'll give him a course of multivitamins—you look as if you could do with them, Michael—and we might send him down for a blood test, as well. All right, Mrs. Devine?"

"Yes, of course."

The doctor leaned back.

"Apart from that, Michael, try to get some exercise and don't study too hard." He took a pen from his desk and began to scribble. "These are the pills to get," he said slowly, "and here's your referral. It's Selby Lane; you know the place? I'll call them for you, and you can pop down straight away. All right?"

"Yes, Doctor, thank you," said Mrs. Devine. Michael trailed her out of the surgery.

"A *blood test*?" he wailed, out on the street.

"Michael, be sensible, for goodness' sake."

"But—" Michael cast about for arguments. "He *said* I wasn't sick . . ."

"Well, I suppose you could have an iron deficiency or something. Really, Michael! You'll be out in five minutes."

"Hmm," Michael growled, feeling very hard done by. Why did life have to be so complicated! "Where is it?"

"Selby Lane, he said. You don't need me, do you? You're quite old enough to go by yourself. I've got some shopping to do."

Go on, thought Michael, desert me. Leave me to my fate.

"Yes, all right," he said.

"Have you got money?"

"No."

"Then take this," said Mrs. Devine, pushing some notes into his hand. "And I'll see you at home, all right? Michael?"

"Yes," said Michael, preoccupied. "Okay, Gran."

They parted company.

———

Down Selby Lane, it was an eternally dull day. Forged between two shop-fronted buildings, it seemed all pavement and drains, the sort of alleyway where footsteps and the loose coughs of small children seemed to echo on forever. The pathologist's, with its polished metal plate beside the door, was about halfway down—between the office for the local paper and the dentist's. Sighing, Michael approached the door, lifted his hand to knock, and heard:

"I wouldn't go in there if I were you."

She was standing on the corner, very calm, gazing at him through the dullness of the alley. Michael stared briefly, then looked over his shoulder and sauntered over to her.

"Good," she said, coolly appreciative. She pulled him a little way around the corner, into a small damp gap with gray garbage cans lined up along the opposite wall. "Good," she repeated, more softly.

"Why shouldn't I go in?" asked Michael carefully.

"Because They are after you. And I think They are in there."

"Oh, Them," said Michael, profoundly.

The girl stood with her back against the wall, very upright, hands clasped in front. She was wearing a dark-colored coat with padded shoulders and a small brooch on the lapel, and something about her reminded Michael of some of the photos he had seen of his mother, when she was young. "But I have to go in," he insisted, confused.

"Then go in," she said. "But keep on your toes. I'm here to give you something They will probably want."

She took a small card from her pocket and handed it to him.

Michael looked at it. "But there's nothing on it," he said.

"Nothing for you."

"Well—who do I give it to, then?"

She smiled. "The Sparrow, of course."

Then, suddenly, she pushed him into the shadows. Michael, flattening himself obediently against the wall, waited. And, just for a moment, he thought he heard footsteps passing. But he saw nothing, and presently she relaxed and smiled coolly at him.

"What was that in aid of?" said Michael.

"Oh," she said, a little surprised. "Don't you know him? SS, of course. He got one of us, last week. I must go. Good luck. And *SEI* . . ."

She faded into the shadows.

———

Michael shivered, shut his eyes, and thought, hard.

How, how was he to take her? He didn't feel like disregarding her; she had given him a warning. But then, if she was seeing SS agents walking down Selby Lane, perhaps her advice simply wasn't relevant. Perhaps she was just some sort of—*ghost*.

Ghost.

But he had to go in. The doctor had called and all. If he didn't turn up, Gran would find out and there would be hell to pay. And he would only have to go again, some other day. Besides, the girl hadn't exactly said not to. And after all, as Michael was beginning to fear, she might only have been in his imagination.

Michael stood, in an agony of indecision. Then he remembered the card. He pawed through his pockets and after a moment hit upon something cool and cardboard. It existed, white and blank as before. So she was real. But her warning . . .

Michael shoved the card back into his pocket, took out the doctor's referral, and marched out into the lane. This was ridiculous. So long as the card was kept safe for the Sparrow—and *any* fool—

He opened the door and approached the reception desk.

"I've got an appointment," he said. "I'm Michael Devine."

"And whose patient are you, Michael?"

The nurse, young and pink, leaning over to write in a large, flat notebook, smiled at him. Michael smiled back and wished he didn't feel so sick.

"Er—Doctor Barratt—"

"Good. Now, I'll just show you in—she'll have a look at you right away, I think."

She led him to a door at the end of a short hallway and opened it for him. Michael went in.

At first, he didn't understand. It was like a practical joke, really. But then he thought, she must be new and she's opened the wrong door. For it was quite dark—stuffy like a closet, and—Michael spun around to call her back.

But he couldn't find the door.

Then, as his eyes began to get used to the light, he saw that it was a lot bigger than he'd thought. It was like a room, and yet curiously indistinct, as if it had no walls. In the middle was a sort of table, and someone stood leaning over it, staring at him. But Michael could hardly see her; afterward he couldn't even say what had made him think it was a woman. And it wasn't only the darkness. The person herself seemed blurred.

"It's the note I want," she said softly. "Could I have it, please?"

Michael squinted into the darkness.

"Who are you?"

"That doesn't matter. I want the note, please. If you hand it over, you may go. It's more important than you are at the moment."

Michael's heart plunged like a swallow in flight.

"I—I don't know what you mean . . ."

"Just give it to me, there's a good boy. It can hold no further interest for you."

"But it's not *mine* . . ."

"Well, then, it should be returned to its rightful owner. Come along."

Michael, confused, moved forward a little way.

"Yes. I mean, no. You don't understand. I—"

"We can keep you here forever, you know, and no one will ever know. Time cannot advance until you leave this place."

She came slowly around the table. Michael, suddenly galvanized into action, ducked and swapped places with her. But the scene did not change. The view was exactly the same from both sides of the table.

Michael stared into the blur in front of him. *Time could not advance*—but that wasn't possible. He—he had come through a door—he was supposed to be in an office—this place could *not* exist—

She darted suddenly after him, and he slid again around the table. Then he knew what to do. He had only to concentrate.

Michael, ignoring everything, stood stiffly in the middle of nowhere. *This does not exist. The door was open. I have only to go on in . . .*

"Ah, Michael, is it?" The pathologist looked up pleasantly. "Just sit down on the couch, here . . ."

He was out in five minutes.

―――――

But it was a long way home.

Pausing at the corner, Michael tried very hard to get himself in hand. His thoughts were whirling so hard and fast that he felt dizzy. And the main street, with its shops and its people, stretched out before him. He had to get home.

So Michael walked slowly down the street, trying to forget the creeping feeling in his spine. As his eyes slid uncomfortably from side to side, he found himself shrinking from the people around him—the mothers and paperboys and blue-shirted men—even the old ladies standing in the warm, sweet blast of the cake shop doorway. This, he supposed dimly, was the War. Panic mounted within him.

Then he stopped in front of the butcher's. He was being stupid. It was only a shopping center, after all. Nothing could hurt him out here. Taking deep breaths, he watched as the fat pink hands of the butcher drew a string of sausages from the window, and was suddenly sickened by the sight of all that red, raw meat.

It was no use. As he walked away, he could not dispel the feeling that he was being followed. It was irrational, he thought irritably. There were plenty of perfectly normal people around, and no real reason to think anyone was following him. But there it was: a coldness in the small of his back, a shadow on his mind.

Michael walked quickly, weaving through hordes of eyes he could not meet and trying to think of something sensible to do. He could feel the panic rising in his throat, and he knew he was about to break into a run. He didn't want to do it; he knew he would tire too quickly, and then . . .

But Michael began to run. He couldn't help it. And he was certain someone was running behind him. His heart thudded painfully in his chest; the street blurred before his eyes.

Then, just as he thought all was lost, he felt a coolness wash over him. The simple solution clicked into place. He ducked smoothly into an arcade, slipped around the corner, and leaned up close against the solid brick building of the bank. He watched the street, holding his breath. But no one had followed.

Michael, weak with relief, sighed deeply. Then felt a light hand on his shoulder.

It was the Sparrow.

"I'm sorry," he said calmly. "Did I frighten you?"

Michael just smiled wanly and handed him the card.

The Sparrow looked at it. "Good," he said softly, and his image wavered, so that for a moment Michael could barely see him. Michael, however, was beginning to get used to this. He watched quietly as the Sparrow finished reading the note, but started when it disappeared.

"Oh—"

"Don't ask."

Michael swallowed. "All right. But—can I—"

"Go on."

"Well, it's the Swanningwren . . ."

The Sparrow, cool and handsome in his dark suit, smiled. "Didn't you know you got her through?"

"*Me?* But . . ."

A lady, coming out of the bank and passing them hurriedly, gave the Sparrow what is called a funny look. The Sparrow looked faintly embarrassed.

"Come on, Devine," he said. "Perhaps we'd better get you home."

They kept to the back streets.

"Could—could I ask you something?" said Michael after a minute or two. "How, exactly, did I help her—the Swanningwren?"

The Sparrow ducked his head and peered upward at him.

"Just by feeling for her," he said. "Your sympathy was enough to open her way."

Michael stored that away, for further consideration.

"I—I didn't know it—the War, I mean—had anything to do with magic."

The Sparrow studied him. "The fact is, Devine," he

said carefully, "there is very little that the Secret War *hasn't* got something to do with."

"But how can you drag the *past* into it?" asked Michael quickly.

The Sparrow smiled his sudden pink and white smile.

"The girl who gave you the card, you mean? But I've told you, Devine. The Secret War has no time or place— it is everywhere, always, for everyone. This, Devine, is a war that cuts across time and place—and even," he added softly, "even identity. Do you understand?"

He stopped, and Michael looked up to find he was home. The Sparrow, smiling a little sadly, looked at him with cool gray eyes.

"You don't, do you?"

"What?"

"Understand."

"No," said Michael.

"But you will," said the Sparrow. He glanced at the emerald green thing on his wrist. "By the way, I must congratulate you on this afternoon. You were excellent." To Michael's surprise he reached out to shake his hand. And, with a flutter and sigh, was gone.

———

"There's nothing to drink," said Michael, peering into the fridge and rescuing Jilly's geometry set from the vegetable drawer.

Mrs. Devine, switching on the kitchen light, looked up distractedly.

"Why don't you have something healthy, for a change?" she said, looking on critically as Robyn modeled Jilly's old party dress. "It's not really as long as we thought, is it, Robyn?"

"It's awful," said Robyn flatly.

Jilly appeared on the stairs.

"Has anyone seen my—? Oh, Michael, what'd they say?"

"It's too *short*," said Robyn.

"Not very much," said Michael.

"But there's quite a hem on it," said Mrs. Devine. "We could let it down—"

"When d'you get the results back?" said Jilly.

"But, Gran," said Robyn. "Even if it was longer—"

"They usually call, don't they?" said Mrs. Devine. "Honestly, Robyn, it's not the West End—"

"I bet nothing shows," said Michael. "It's on the table, Jilly."

"What's it doing there, I wonder? Thanks, Mike," said Jilly, tucking the geometry set under her arm. She looked at Robyn with her head on one side. "Doesn't really look very princessy, does it?"

"Oh, don't you start," said Mrs. Devine.

And Robyn's lip began to wobble.

"Here we go," sighed Michael.

"Well," Robyn began, winding up, "so would *you* be upset. How can I do anything properly in *this*? E-everyone'll *laugh* . . ."

Michael, giving up the fridge as a bad job, went to the sink to get a glass of water. Grimacing, he wondered what would happen next and whether it got worse or better as you went along.

"Don't get upset," said Jilly. "We'll find something."

"Something!" cried Robyn. "*Something!*"

She stamped her foot.

"Now, Rob—" began Mrs. Devine warningly.

"If I'm going to look like this, I may as well be the *witch*!"

44

"Now there's an idea," said Michael. "Why don't you audition?"

For a moment, she just stared at him. "You—you—" she stammered. "You—" She burst into tears. And stomped out.

Jilly gazed at him reproachfully. The kettle began to wheeze, and she switched it off.

"You are out of sorts, lately," said Mrs. Devine.

"*Me?*" said Michael. "What about *her?*"

"Well," comforted Jilly, "at least she's got it out of her system. If she has a good cry, she'll be right as rain in the morning."

"Hmm," said Michael, dubiously. It had struck him again. That feeling that all this somehow fitted together, in a pattern he couldn't quite make out. *Without time or place . . .*

"What'd you say?" said Jilly.

"Nothing," said Michael, already halfway down the stairs.

"Oh, by the way," called Jilly, "Sarah Jane's coming to dinner tomorrow night. I thought you might—"

"All right!" yelled Michael.

But he hadn't really heard her.

Enter Sarah Jane

The Thursday after the mirror cracked grew into a sweet, sunny afternoon, in which Michael, just home from school, felt positively uncomfortable. For the day, like many of its type before he had let the War enter his life, had been singularly uneventful. True, there had been a math test on a chapter he hadn't even looked at, and a few more than usually unkind comments from his friends about cutting—but they were normal things. And after yesterday, the Secret War had been strangely quiet.

Michael was *not* glad of the rest. It was less nerve-racking when things were actually happening. But, as he dragged himself up the stairs with his gray school sweater tied by the sleeves around his waist, he hadn't long to wait.

Finding nothing, as usual, in the fridge, Michael wrote JUNKY DRINK on his grandmother's shopping list (without much hope) and got himself a glass of water. Then he wandered into the living room, where the afternoon sunlight fell in latticed patches on the carpet, and lay down on the floor. He locked his hands behind his neck, gazed up at the ceiling and thought.

"Lying on the floor in your uniform again," sighed

46

Robyn loftily, coming out of her pink and white bedroom. "Gran says *mud* came out of your shirt in the wash yesterday."

"Shut up," said Michael, without malice.

"You're just like a dog, really," Robyn pursued, inspired. "The minute you get something clean on your back you have to go and *roll* in it."

"It's a wonder you're not after *me* with the Zap'em," said Michael.

"I haven't noticed any fleas," said Robyn speculatively. "I'd better talk to Jilly about it, though. Which reminds me, Mikey—avoid the new cake at all costs."

"What's wrong with it?"

"Oh, you know—Jilly's Secret Recipe—i.e., If-I-let-anyone - know - what's - in - it - they - wouldn't - touch - it - with-a-ten-foot-pole. Guess what Miss Thom said."

"What?"

" 'I wish everyone could read like you, Robyn.' "

"Really?" said Michael, thinking, *without time or place* . . .

"I'm still annoyed with you," said Robyn. "It might not look like it, but I am. And I'm *not* wearing that dress, whatever Gran says."

"You tell 'em, love."

"Well, it's not *fair*."

"Yes, but you haven't got much choice, have you?"

Robyn glared.

"I'd rather wear my uniform," she said vehemently.

"Michael," said Mrs. Devine, appearing suddenly in the doorway, "for heaven's sake, get off the floor. No wonder your shirts get so grubby."

Robyn snickered. Michael got up obediently and squinted at his grandmother's distracted face.

"What's up?" he asked her.

"Nothing for dinner," she said, biting her lip. "Look, d'you think you two might pop down to the shops for me?"

"All right," said Michael, wandering into the kitchen, half-listening as Mrs. Devine expounded the details of the shopping list.

" . . . but not the thick sort, we can't fit that in the machine. Now . . . butter, ice cream, bananas, a *large* can of pineapple, please—"

"Could I have an aspirin, please, Devine?" said the Sparrow, suddenly behind him.

"Yes, of course," said Michael. "In the cupboard to your right—yeah, that's it. You're supposed to take two of those, I think—"

And Robyn, halfway out the door, called, "Coming, Mike?"

———

They divided up the list, according to which side of the street the right shops stood on, and arranged to meet at the pine trees. But as Michael, laden with various items, approached the particular seat where stray Devines always met up, he remembered that Robyn generally took ages, and prepared himself for a long wait. He sat on the green-painted wooden bench, chosen for the view it had of the whispering sea, and gazed out over the water. The sun was very low in the sky—some clouds had begun to color—and the birds in the long row of pine trees behind him were chattering raucously of the day's doings. Michael, sighing deeply, felt that he could tolerate a *very* late Robyn quite well . . .

He didn't know what it was that made him sit up, or even when, exactly, it happened. But the first strange thing he actually noticed was the sea gull. It seemed, quite suddenly, to have increased dramatically in size. It was *gigantic,* for a sea gull. But then Michael realized that it wasn't a sea gull at all. It was a swan.

Michael blinked, stared, and then noticed to his considerable surprise that the sea had disappeared. Before him, instead, was what looked like a lake, surrounded by blue-green grass and bordered with tall, reedy-looking plants. On a distant shore stood a building that resembled the pictures Michael had seen of medieval castles—and, not far from him, standing, staring out over the lake, was a lady.

She had long silvery hair and was holding a gray cloak around her. On her head was a coronet woven of flowers, and her gown was white, very loose and simple, bound around the waist with a gold chain. She was very slender, almost childlike, and somewhat frail-looking. But she was breathtaking.

Michael half-stood, and then sat down again. The lady turned.

"Hello, friend," said a voice like the wind through the pine trees.

Michael crept toward her.

"Who—who are you?" he whispered.

The lady smiled, as if she saw an infinite complexity in the question, but answered simply, "I am Deirdre."

Michael just stared. "C-can I help you?" he said at last, feeling ludicrously like a sales assistant. "I—er—"

"A friend can always help at a time of testing. And my hour is near."

"Your—I don't . . ."

Deirdre looked at him. "As the sun sets," she sighed, "I must drink this." She showed him a tiny crystal bottle, filled with clear liquid.

Michael blinked. "Why must you?" he said. "What is it? You don't have to do anything if you don't want to."

"Ah," said Deirdre, "but I do want to. I am only a little fearful—now, when the time is so near."

"What will it do?" Michael asked again.

"Help me accomplish my mission," said Deirdre simply. "Are you from far away, my friend?"

"No, not far," said Michael, gesturing vaguely back at the bench. "Are you in the War, too?"

Deirdre smiled softly.

"In my way," she said. She unfastened the cloak, which Michael hastened to take from her. The sun was already staining the clouds. Deirdre paused, and said: "Would you give him a message for me? Would you tell him *SEI* from Deirdre?"

"Hmm?" Michael grunted, watching helplessly as she unstoppered the bottle. "T-tell *who*?"

Deirdre looked at the bottle in her hand, then glanced up at him. "The Sparrow, of course," she said, and drank.

It was as if she were melting. For a moment she was all a blur, shrinking, sinking slowly to the grass. Then there was a little breeze, a whirring, and a white swan flying onto the lake. It gazed at him through its black mask, and then rose with a flutter from the water and flew off into the dusk. Michael, his arms full of cloak, gazed after it.

And Robyn, all agog, cried:

"*Golly!* What's this?"

Michael started.

"Eh?"

She was holding up the white dress, with the hem dangling on the grass, pressing it to her small breast. It gave her face a curious sort of glow. Michael blinked at her.

"Wherever did it come from?" she squealed.

"I—er—found it," said Michael.

"I can't believe it!" cried Robyn. "It's perfect for the Princess!"

Michael felt his knees weaken.

"For—for the *what*?" he said faintly.

"Was the cloak there with it?"

"Er—"

"We'll have to take it home with us. We can't just leave it here."

"No," said Michael, rubbing a hand over his eyes. "I s'pose not."

"Just wait till I show Gran! Golly, it's a good thing you saw it there! How lucky can you get!"

"Er—Rob—"

"Come *on*, Michael!"

Cradling arms full of dress and groceries, she was already way ahead of him. Michael gathered up the cloak and started out after her. He felt oddly close to tears. But what really confused him was the presence of Deirdre's clothes. He had always thought the two worlds—his own and that of the Secret War—to be quite distinct from one another. But now, for the first time, he was conscious of an overlapping. And if Robyn could really wear that dress in a school play, perhaps the two worlds were not so separate after all.

Juliet, blue-eyed and kind in her white shirt and green plaid school skirt, met them on the stairs.

"It's *beautiful!*" she exclaimed.

"Michael found it," gasped Robyn. "In the park."

"In the *park?*" Jilly gazed at him with a half a smile. "Whoever could've left it there?"

"Finders keepers," said Robyn quickly.

"Well, I don't know," said Jilly, "you'd better ask Gran."

Robyn, suddenly worried, gathered up the dress and dived upstairs. Michael sat down on the stairs.

"You hungry, at all?" said Jilly, eyeing him in a maternal fashion.

"What's for dinner?"

"Well," said Jilly, "whatever you brought home, most likely. What *did* you bring home?"

"Canned ham," said Michael. "Potato salad. Quick stuff, mainly. We in a hurry?"

"We got into a bit of a muddle," said Jilly, "because of Sarah Jane—"

"*Who?*"

"Sarah Jane Yardley. You know, the little one I'm supposed to be coaching. Gran reckons I didn't say anything about dinner, but I'm sure I—"

"*Dinner?*" said Michael.

"Mike, I told you about this yesterday. Don't you remember?"

Michael buried his face in the cloak. "Can't you say I'm sick?"

Jilly was mystified.

"Michael, she's only a kid. She shouldn't bother you— she's very nice."

But it wasn't that. And Jilly should've known, thought Michael obscurely. *No one* understood.

"I'm going downstairs," he muttered. And was beginning to gather up the cloak again when someone appeared on the landing.

"Juliet," she said gravely. "I'm finished." And then she looked, very candidly, at Michael.

Michael started.

She was dressed in the bottle-green pinafore and white shirt that was the junior uniform of Jilly's beloved school. A very long, dark braid hung down her back, and her hair, middle parted, framed a vivid, pointed little face. Her eyes, which were the misty gray of the sea on a rainy morning, were catlike and fringed with thick, dark lashes. But what Michael saw in her was the oddest thing—a certain look of the Sparrow. He got up and looked quickly away from her.

"This is my brother Michael," Jilly was saying. "Michael, this is Sarah Jane Yardley."

"Hello, Michael."

"Hello, Sparrow," said Michael, without thinking.

He almost died.

But Jilly, looking at her pupil's exercises, appeared not to have heard. Only Sarah Jane, gazing at him, seemed to take the meaning.

"That's my favorite bird," she remarked.

Jilly, saying something about irregular verbs, hustled her back upstairs.

———

At dinner, Michael made sure to sit as far away from Sarah Jane Yardley as possible. He wanted to watch.

"But, *Gran*," Robyn protested, helping herself distractedly to slices of ham, "who would *want* them?"

"If you want them, someone else might," said Mrs. Devine reasonably. "Be fair, Robyn."

"But they haven't got names on them, or anything . . ."

"Yes," said moral Jilly, "but you'd want whoever lost them to have them back, wouldn't you?"

Quite plainly, this was not the case.

"Robyn," said Mrs. Devine, "we must at least put an ad in the paper. It wouldn't be fair, dear. They look valuable."

"But they'd be *perfect* for the play," said Robyn, with a certain edge in her voice. "And *I* found them."

"If you're going by finders keepers," said Jilly, "they're actually Mike's."

"Well, same thing," said Robyn, as suddenly miserable as she had been ecstatic. She was like that.

And Mrs. Devine said: "I wonder whoever would lose a thing like that?"

"The fairies," said Sarah Jane.

Michael looked up, looked away, and flushed. Jilly laughed.

"Anyway," said Mrs. Devine, "I don't want you touching them until we can be reasonably sure they're abandoned. It'd be dreadful if you spilled something on them."

"But I *wouldn't*," said Robyn indignantly. "I wouldn't, Gran, really . . ."

And Michael, thinking suddenly of Deirdre, was almost overwhelmed. He swallowed firmly and looked away from the table. It struck him that he had discovered a new part of himself, deep inside and perpetually red-raw. This sympathy business was painful.

"But why don't you ask them?" said Jilly.

Robyn looked up.

"What d'you mean?"

"Well, whoever owns it probably has something to do with the theater. If they get in touch, you could ask them if they'd lend it to you, just for the play. People do that, you know."

Robyn gave a sort of yelp.

"You're a *genius!*"

"Robyn," said Mrs. Devine.

"But, Gran, don't you see? Now everything is all right—"

"Just eat, Robyn."

And Michael, who had been deep in thought, was suddenly visited by a vision of Deirdre answering a notice in the Lost and Found. He looked up, smiling, and accidentally caught the sea-gray glance of Sarah Jane Yardley. They smiled briefly at one another, as if at a private joke, then quickly looked away.

Then, just as Michael had decided to give up dinner as another bad job, there came a brisk knock on the door.

"Oh, that'll be your father, Sarah," said Mrs. Devine.

"I'll go and see," said Jilly, and went to answer it.

But Michael knew the voice was not Mr. Yardley's. Excusing himself, he decided to be very helpful and take some plates out to the kitchen. You could hear better, from there . . .

"Oh," said Jilly's voice, with a blush in it, "I—er—expected someone else. I'll get Gran   "

"No, don't bother." Simon's voice seemed almost nervous. "I'm just bringing back the keys. Could you tell Mrs. Devine I think she's got white ants?"

"Oh, heavens, where?"

"Downstairs," said Simon, matter-of-factly. "It's a wonder Michael hasn't heard them."

"That's probably why he can't sleep," Jilly murmured.

"Oh, doesn't he?" said Simon, not surprised. "Poor bloke."

Get off *me*, thought Michael impatiently. But it was all right—

"I—er—saw your cards in the handicraft shop," Jilly was saying hesitantly. "I think they're marvelous. Especially the tone."

Simon, a little more hopeful, said: "You paint, too, don't you?"

"Well," said Jilly, "not *really* . . ."

Honestly, thought Michael.

"If ever I could—er—be of any help—" Simon began, his voice sounding odd because he never said things like that, "feel free . . ."

And Mrs. Devine, coming into the hall, said: "Oh, it's you, Simon."

The subject, from then on, was white ants.

After a moment, Jilly excused herself and escaped into the kitchen. There, without noticing a silent Michael at the sink, she sank onto a chair and covered her face with her hands.

Walking on Thin Ice

On Friday morning, Michael awoke with a headache and the frustrating conviction that he had missed the bus. And so he had. The little clock on his cracked dressing table leered 8:40; the bus left from the bottom of the hill at 8:30. He had forgotten to set the alarm.

Michael was superstitiously sure it was an omen. Cursing to himself, he pawed through the jungle that was his desk, threw his pajama shirt at the clock, which had unaccountably begun to tinkle, and was just coming across a clean pair of socks under his bed, when:

"Oh, Michael, you slept in," said Jilly's gentle voice, as her head peeped in round the door.

"I know," said Michael.

"Gran says you mustn't go without breakfast," said Jilly, patting on her hat—the convent's green panama. "And by the way, you're right about *The Dam Busters.* It's quite risky, reading it on the train, though. You get all excited, and people look—"

"What d'you do, jump up and down or something?"

"No, just giggle. Especially during the radio bits. Anyway, see you this afternoon."

And she was gone.

Michael, sighing, pulled on a shirt. He hated being late. They made you go into chapel, anyway, and if everyone was already sitting down, you looked so devastatingly conspicuous. And Michael was one of those who like always to keep a low profile. He was in the firm habit of watching *other* people make fools of themselves; he wasn't used to having it the other way around—even in something quite trivial. He felt like spitting.

Luckily, however, his grandmother was not in the flat. Which meant, at least, skipping breakfast in peace. Knotting his tie, he gulped coffee, splashed his face at the kitchen sink, and flattened his hair with his hands. That was Michael's version of being ready for school. Feeling better, he hopped back downstairs, grabbed his schoolbag, and ventured into the street.

It was quite a walk, without the bus—down the hill, through the shopping center, and up the long slope that ran alongside the football field. Michael, with his bag over his shoulder and one hand in his pocket, stalked it bravely. Until, at the base of the second slope, something happened.

It was in the last reaches of the shopping center, in a back street behind Selby Lane, that Michael heard the noises. And he found the culprits in the alley between the real estate agent's and the pet shop. There were about eight or ten of them, little kids, really—and they were making life very unpleasant for something or other up at the end of the alley. It was early; the shops hadn't opened yet, and there was nobody about. Michael, peering uncertainly into the din at the end of the alley, felt a sudden coldness in his spine.

If you had asked him at any time what he hated most in the world, Michael would most likely have answered

58

by describing the type of situation he was watching just now. He had a horror of bullying. Certain experiences, in the year after his parents had died, had left him with a sort of personal vendetta against it—and this, to the embarrassment of his friends, and often to his own disadvantage, he was constantly putting into effect.

"Hey!" he yelled in his most authoritative manner. "What d'you kids think you're doing?"

Michael had been prepared for an argument, at least. But no argument was necessary. They were *terrified*.

Amazed, he jumped out of the way. They swarmed past him, out into the street and into obscurity, yelping like little—

But they weren't kids at all. Faces, little, wizened faces, black-eyed and canine, rushed past him, leaving a horrible impression of wickedness and fear that would be hard to forget. The last of them scuttled down to the end of the alley, yapping, and disappeared.

Michael sank back against the wall.

It was some minutes before he could rouse himself sufficiently to peer into the darkness at the end of the alley, searching out the victim. When he saw him, Michael gasped.

Half kneeling, half squatting, he was coolly inspecting what appeared to be a wound in his upper arm. No blood, however, showed on the faultless black of his suit—and indeed he seemed scarcely the worse for wear. Only his face was paler beneath the shock of fair hair, and when he looked up at Michael, his gray eyes were bleak.

"Do you have a handkerchief, by any chance?" he said.

Michael, pulling everything *but* a handkerchief out of his pockets, stumbled over.

"I—I had no idea—"

Finally he found one in his blazer. The Sparrow, snatching it from him, tied a quick knot with his teeth around his arm and looked up at Michael.

"Thank you," he said. "I hope you can manage without it." He held out his hand.

"Yes, of *course*," Michael said, pulling him up obediently. "Are you sure—"

"I'm all right, Devine. Now listen. You have helped me, and today will be dangerous for you. You must take care, and keep calm. Do you understand?"

Michael eyed him dubiously.

"Who *were* they?"

"That you need never know. I am not here to relieve your curiosity." He went to glance at the green thing on his wrist, but winced violently as he moved his arm. Then he looked at Michael and softened. "I'm sorry," he said.

"That's all right," said Michael. "Listen—I've got a message . . ."

The Sparrow looked up.

"Yes?"

"Just—just *SEI*, from Deirdre."

"Oh," said the Sparrow. He paused for a moment, thoughtful. Then he smiled a little sadly. "Thank you, Devine. Good luck."

And, with a flutter and sigh, was gone.

———

Michael's school—a prim, spare, tree-lined set of buildings—sat at the summit of a rambling slope. What people called the chapel was more of an assembly hall, really—equipped with baby grand, flowers, and a silver crucifix on a table. Michael, who could see into it along the last stretch of his walk, noted with dread that everyone had gone in. So he would have to go in late.

It was all he needed. With the Sparrow's words spinning round uncomfortably in his head, he braved the last of the long slope and approached the outside entrance.

If you were late, you came in through one of the glass doors along the side. Michael dumped his bag, ducked his head, and sneaked in past the front row of gaping first formers. He was about to tiptoe down into the comparative safety of his own class, when, as he genuflected hurriedly, he felt an authoritative hand on his shoulder.

Flannagan.

"Yes, sir?"

"Here, thank you, Devine."

So he sank resignedly into the blasted space (just big enough) between Flannagan and the nearest first former. All hope of inconspicuous comfort fled from him. But things could be worse, he supposed. He was right. For Flannagan was tone-deaf. And he seemed to be the only one in the immediate vicinity who wasn't actually aware of the fact. Unfortunately, Michael, as they stood to sing the Lord's Prayer, was not so happily ignorant.

It didn't seem funny, at first, just a pain. But as they reached some of the higher bits, something dreadful happened to Michael. He began to giggle.

It was horrifying. His shoulders shook, his eyes streamed with water, and he was stiff with the effort of trying to stop. But there seemed no hope. Desperate, he pressed a fist to his mouth and tried to think about something else—and if *only* Flannagan wasn't so busy singing, he might send him out, for anything was better than—

61

But suddenly, they were singing *Amen,* and sitting down again. Michael, weak with relief, collapsed against the wooden back of his seat. Then:

"*Devine*," echoed a microphoned voice. "If you're quite finished enjoying the joke, perhaps you could tell me what you're doing down the front?"

Michael crimsoned, struck dumb. He was vaguely aware of Flannagan's making explanatory noises beside him, but heard only:

"Late, eh? See me after, thank you."

And he knew what that meant.

———

Being late was one thing. Disrupting chapel was another. But setting such a disgusting example to the younger boys was insufferable. Michael had a good record; it was surprising and disappointing to have to treat him like a first former. He had always *thought* Michael was the responsible type. This episode would not be repeated, it was to be hoped.

Michael half-listened, staring at the asphalt outside the hall, and tried to ignore the members of his form as they filed past him and on up to math. This was going to be one of those days.

"Do you understand?"

"Yes, Father."

"Very well, then. Off you go."

The fact that he had to have math first that day and that the teacher had to be Flynn, who had just ticked him off, seemed extraordinarily bad luck.

"But what was the matter with you?" Paul demanded, leaning on the opposite desk with his hands in his pockets. Michael, in frantic search of his homework, emptied the contents of his briefcase onto his desk.

"You know," he said, throwing books around, "when you can't stop laughing—"

"Yes," said Paul, "but I've never seen you like that before. Gee, you've been strange, lately."

"Look, don't you start, all right?"

"What d'you mean, don't *me* start? If you're turning maniac, you may as well know it."

Michael, who couldn't even begin to explain, just muttered:

"I was a teenage maniac."

Which made him laugh, at least. Then, subject dropped, he buried his head in his desk. Flynn was funny about homework.

The classroom hummed cheerfully for a further two minutes, then fell silent as Father Flynn made his entrance.

"Last night's homework, please" were his opening lines.

And Michael, to the amusement of the class, decided there was nothing for it but to go on looking. Father Timothy Flynn prowled the room.

"Where's yours then, Millowski?"

"Left it at home, Father."

"I'll see it first thing tomorrow morning, then, and I think another go at Set H wouldn't do you any harm." Flynn leaned over, scribbled on an exercise book. "Your problem's concentration, Dowd. Not bad, Phillips." And a pause. "All right, Banks, what's *that*?"

Michael, sighing, began to make systematic piles of every exercise book he owned—except his math homework. This *was* one of those days.

Black trousers stopped beside him.

"I take it you've lost yours, Devine?"

The class tittered. Michael would murder them all, one by one, at recess.

"Yes, Father," he sighed.

"I've already seen you once, today, Devine. Not your day, is it?"

"No, Father."

"Well, I think you could do with another go at chapter thirteen. That test of yours was a very poor effort. I want to see D, E, F, and G on my table tomorrow, thank you. And if they're well done, you needn't bother with A, B, and C. All right?"

It *was* a bad test. Eleven out of twenty. No wonder.

Michael, incapable of following the lesson, swung on his chair and gazed at the front in what he hoped to be an attentive manner.

The Sparrow, apparently, could be hurt.

It seemed stupid, now, that he had never thought of it before. He had simply assumed that the Sparrow was more or less invincible. And, in particular, that nothing very bad could happen to him, while the Sparrow was around. But if the Sparrow could be hurt . . .

Michael frowned at the board. He was a Helper, wasn't he? And he was supposed to be helping, in a way he did not fully understand, through what the Sparrow called sympathy. All the same, he was still only Michael Devine—and what if he'd caught the bus as usual this morning? What if he hadn't passed that alley? What if the Sparrow had been—

Killed?

The chair stopped swinging. Michael balancing on the two back legs, leaned against the desk behind him.

Killed?

And then, quite suddenly, Michael knew what it meant, to be in the War. It wasn't kids' stuff. It wasn't some harmless storybook adventure. They meant business, whoever or whatever, They were. They were out to get the Sparrow. They had nearly killed the Swanningwren.

But where did that leave Michael?

One thing was certain: They didn't want him helping. *Were They after him, too?*

The back legs scraped against the floorboards, and suddenly he was a sprawling heap. Michael, stunned, gazed around him as the class went into merciless hysterics.

"Get out, Devine."

Michael, burning all over, righted his chair and shuffled out of the classroom. Paul, watching his progress, shuddered.

———

His friends, shuffling out of the room and on up to French, jostled him sympathetically. Flynn, however, was not so kind.

"You're what we call a disruptive element, Devine. And I've had about enough from you this morning. Come on, son."

He bounded off down the hall. Michael, trotting behind him, stammcrcd:

"Wh-where're we going?"

Father Flynn screamed around the corner.

"To the Principal, of course."

Michael almost passed out.

"B-but, Father—"

For you were only sent to the Principal for something

65

positively delinquent—not piffling offenses like lateness, or giggling, or losing your homework, or falling off your chair. Michael, alarmed, was suddenly aware that something, somewhere, was not quite right.

"F-Father?"

Flynn's face, as he tore up the corridor, was ruddy with rage. Dismayed, Michael followed him, wondering whatever to do. This was a terrible mistake. Should he pretend to be ill? He certainly felt it. And Flynn was— not himself. It just wasn't fair. But it wasn't until the Principal's office was inescapably approaching, that Michael thought: Could They *use* people?

And by then it was too late.

"Come in," said the voice.

Flynn stuck his head in, said a few words, gave Michael a shove, and disappeared.

"Ah, Devine. Sit down."

The office, modern and usually not very intimidating, seemed to gape before him. Michael, his heart racing, obeyed.

"Er—Father—"

The Principal looked up.

"How are you, Devine?"

Michael checked. He seemed somehow different.

"All right, thank you," he answered after a moment. "I—er—"

"No problems at home?"

"Problems?" said Michael. "No—I—"

"You have been acting a little strangely lately, though. As if you were under some sort of extra strain, eh?"

Michael looked up sharply.

"I don't think so, Father."

But the Principal only chuckled to himself.

"You know, Devine," he said, leaning forward, "if there was anything wrong, anything worrying you, we'd want to know."

"Er—yes—"

"So we could *help* you, of course. That's what we're here for, after all. We try to show you the way, to pull you out of pits—"

"Out of pits?" said Michael, confused.

"Yes; you know what I mean. Or away from bad company. Or out of—er—certain situations."

Michael heard something click, dimly, in the back of his mind.

"I—I don't know if I—"

"Are you *trying* to be stupid?"

The Principal turned on him, venomous. Michael jumped.

"Yes, I mean, no—"

"Come on, Devine. What exactly is this little game you're playing with us, anyway?"

"I—I don't know what you mean—"

"Oh, don't say that. I thought you were above clichés, Devine. Or have you been watching too many thrillers lately?"

Michael stood, suddenly angry. "Who's playing games now?" he said.

"Very witty," said the Principal. "War is only another sort of game, you know."

Michael paled. "Who are you?" he whispered, staring into the familiar face.

"That does not concern you. I wish only to advise you."

"Advise me?"

"Oh, yes. You'd be surprised how little you know, Devine."

The Principal chuckled.

Michael, closing his eyes, snapped, "Will you cut out that stupid laughter?"

The man at the desk simpered at him. "My dear boy, is that any way to treat your friendly neighborhood headmaster? Have a heart, Devine."

Michael, chancing to look down, found that he'd bitten his fingernail to the quick, and it was beginning to bleed. It hadn't hurt until he'd looked at it. He nursed it in his other hand and said:

"Look, I don't have to take this."

"Perhaps not. But we did warn you."

Michael shook his head. "I can't stop seeing things."

"Oh, can't you? Hasn't your friend ever told you about that?"

"I—I don't—"

"Devine, my dear, you only see because you want to. If you should stop wanting, you would stop seeing. It's as simple as that."

Michael bit his lip.

"And you needn't think you're doing any good. You've had small triumphs, of course, but it's only a matter of time. That mission of his—he can't get it finished, you know, not soon enough. And if he doesn't, he's gone. And if he goes, you will very likely go with him. You're walking on thin ice, Devine."

Michael eyed him mutely.

"Poor dear," said the Principal with a sneer. You're confused!" And he opened the door. "Why don't you go away and think about it?"

Michael, emerging, found Paul in the hallway.

"Hell, you look sick!"

He felt it, too. For there, just coming down the hall, was the Principal, the *real* one. He nodded vaguely at them and disappeared into his office.

"Didn't you see him, after all?" said Paul, amazed.

"No," said Michael, hoarsely. "I didn't."

———

When Michael arrived home that afternoon, Mrs. Beasley was just coming down the stairs.

"Oh, hello, dear," she said. "Have a nice day at school?"

But Michael, thinking about padded cells, didn't see her.

"Well!" said Mrs. Beasley.

"I beg your pardon?" said Simon, coming out of No. 2.

"Oh," said Mrs. Beasley, apologetically. "It's just that boy, again."

"Who? Michael? What's he done now?"

Mrs. Beasley lowered her voice. "In a trance, as usual. I just spoke to him, Mr. Collins, and he didn't even blink."

"Didn't he?" said Simon, looking up after him.

And Jilly, sipping sweet, milky tea in the kitchen, said:

"Michael, you do look rough. Is anything wrong?"

He could only gaze at her, mute, and so she tried another line:

"Have you seen Gran yet?"

"No."

"Well, they called today about your blood test. It's quite all right. Nothing showed, anyway."

"I said it wouldn't."

"Yes. Well . . ."

Michael smiled rather nastily at her. "Is Pollyanna home yet?"

"Robyn, you mean? Yes, I—"

"And the white ants continuing in excellent health, I suppose?"

"What a funny mood you're in," said Jilly uncomfortably. "Are you sure you're all right?"

Michael just looked at her. "I don't know why you bother," he said suddenly.

"Michael, what's wrong?"

Michael smiled. "You shouldn't really ask, you know, Jilly. You don't want to hear."

"That's not true. I—"

"Look, why don't you just bugger off, there's a good girl."

"*Michael!*"

He looked up to find his grandmother standing in the doorway. But he was already too far gone. He said, "Michael this, Michael that. All this bloody concern over our little boy's health. It makes me *sick*, and what's more, it's the biggest bloody farce I ever heard of. As if you care!"

"Michael!" repeated his grandmother, stunned. "Michael, that's not true. We—"

Michael gazed at her. It came to him suddenly that he was fighting on the wrong side. And for a moment, he thought he was going to cry. "I—I'm sorry," he said shakily, after a moment.

And left the room.

Traffic with Saints

Michael was frightened. But there was nowhere to run and nothing tangible to run from. So on Saturday he stayed in bed. And thought.

It was an odd sort of day. He told the family he had a headache, and, between alternate bouts of sleep and worry, Jilly would come down with hot milk and aspirin, or Gran would tell him to go out and get some fresh air, or Robyn would attempt to persuade him to practice lines with her. The headache claim was very nearly valid, by the end of all that. But he did get a fair bit of thinking done. So when he awoke at about 5:00 on Sunday morning, he knew what to do. He would go and see Simon.

Michael, pulling on clothes, went quickly and quietly up the stairs.

The house, in the early-morning gray, seemed only a shade of its normal self. Simon was sitting on his workroom table, in jeans and white sneakers and his usual moth-eaten pullover. But the studio, to Michael, seemed odd. Without the sunlight, which so often lit the latticed windows, he felt as if he were standing in a black and white photograph. Simon looked up and frowned at him.

"Oh, hello," he said. "How're you feeling?"

Michael, gazing out the window, only grunted. He was

wondering, in sudden desperation, whether he shouldn't chicken out. At that moment, anything seemed better than telling someone.

Simon, frowning speculatively at Michael's profile, picked an apple from the sideboard and began to peel it with his pocketknife. After a moment, Michael licked his lips.

"Simon," he began. "I—I think I sort of need a second opinion."

Simon cut a slice from the apple and handed it to him on the knife. Michael, distracted, took it and bit in.

"Oh, yes," said Simon, without expression. "What about? Don't you believe the doctor?"

Michael rolled his eyes. "My bloody health. They're obsessed with it, up there."

"It was your gran who mentioned it. It's the price you pay for eccentricity, Michael. People are bound to think there's something wrong with you."

"Yes, well, there isn't. At least, I don't think there is."

"Let's see if I can make it *easier*," said Simon, being Julie Andrews. "What exactly are you so upset about?"

Michael hadn't realized he looked upset. Under the circumstances, the knowledge depressed him further. He sighed, and said: "I think I'm in trouble."

Simon, handing him another piece of apple, tensed only slightly. "Who with?" he said.

Michael glanced up at him. "That's just it," he said. "I don't know."

Simon frowned. "What've you done, exactly?"

"I—I've been sort of helping someone," said Michael. "He asked me, and so I said I would. But I'm beginning to think I've bitten off more than I can chew and I—well,

I can't really tell you much. It's supposed to be a secret."

"If that's the case, you probably shouldn't be telling me anything at all."

"Yes, I know," said Michael. "Only, I'm desperate."

"I see." Simon sliced into the core. "This person—is he in trouble with the police?"

"I—I don't think so. No, of course he's not."

"Then it's nothing to do with drugs or anything like that?"

"Oh, no," said Michael earnestly. "He—he's not like that—" He had to turn away quickly to blink back the tears. "Sorry," he said, after a moment. "It's just, I don't usually tell people things, and . . ."

"It's all right," said Simon. "But can I ask you something? Why *are* you telling me this, anyway?"

"D'you mean, why didn't I tell Gran or someone?"

"Yes."

Michael paused. "Because," he said distantly, "because they wouldn't understand."

Simon glanced up. "This wouldn't have anything to do with magic, would it?"

"Well, yes, it would, sort of," said Michael apologetically.

Simon smiled his rare, sad smile. "I suppose you think you're going loony?" he said calmly.

The words had an odd effect on Michael. He stiffened, as a memory began to spin through his head:

They'll hurt you, Devine. They'll try to change you. They'll even try to make you think you're losing your mind . . .

Simon, frowning, sliced more apple. "The trouble is," he said, at last, "if you're seeing more than most of us, how can *I* advise *you*? You're the wise one."

Michael blinked. "Then—then you believe . . ."

"You couldn't come out of a thesis on folktales without believing in magic—or, at least, entertaining the possibility." Simon gazed at him keenly. "It must be hard," he went on, "to see things. But you're not mad. Or at least, no madder than I am, since I believe in it, too."

Michael felt quite confused. "I—I had no idea—"

"I really don't see why it should be so surprising," said Simon, sliding off the table, slipping a dust cover from the canvas on the easel. "After all, I spend half my time trying to paint magic. My only problem is I never see any. Apart from your Juliet," he added faintly.

But Michael wasn't listening. Somehow, suddenly, everything was all right. He knew now that he wasn't going mad. The Sparrow had said they would try to hurt him, make him fear just what he *had* been fearing—and if Simon believed in magic, *well* . . .

"I haven't helped you much, I'm afraid."

Michael started. "You have," he said. "Believe me."

And Simon looked at the painting. "If there's anything I can do," he said seriously, "don't hesitate, all right?"

———

Michael, leaping up the stairs and into the flat, found that no one was up yet. He splashed his face at the kitchen sink, drank a quick glass of water, and went in to take the cover off the neurotic budgie. Then it struck him that he was making very good time for 7:30 A.M. Mass, and that he may as well go now as later. So he bounded back down the stairs, pulled on something comparatively decent, and set off down to St. Matthew's.

By the time he got down to the church, he still had

half an hour to spare. There were not many people there, apart from a few old dears praying. As he paused at the bookstall, it occurred to Michael that the choir didn't sing at 7:30 Mass, which meant that the choir stalls, upstairs and at the back, would be empty. And there was a window, upstairs, which had always held a sort of fascination for him. Michael decided to visit it.

It was a small, square, push-out affair, almost at floor-level, at the top of the narrow wooden stairway. Michael had liked it ever since he had come to live in Coleridge about five years ago, and he liked it because of the person in it. He was a tall, thin, brown-clad monk, with a mop of saffron-glass hair, tending a green-glass garden. He was apparently meant to be a saint, but there was only a dedication beneath him, not a word about who he was, which Michael had always found somewhat frustrating. However, the problem that morning, as he weaved toward his window through the choir stalls, was of a more immediate nature. The saint was gone.

It gave him quite a shock, at first. There was the gap, there was the frame, and there was the green glass which usually surrounded him. But the brown-robed figure had vanished from his garden.

"They must've got rid of it," he said aloud. "But how—"

"Rid of what?" said an eager voice.

Michael jumped, turned, and saw a young man sitting in the choir stalls behind him.

"Oh, I'm sorry," he said, surprised. "I thought, I mean, I didn't know . . ." But he fizzled out in wonder. The young man was almost intolerably familiar. "Don't I know you?" he asked, confusedly.

"Yes, I think you do," said the young man, pushing back his yellow hair in a quick, careless manner. "I've known you for years."

Michael frowned at him. "I'm sorry, I—"

"Never mind about that. I want to talk to you about the War. Sit down."

Michael sat. The early-morning sunshine, young and yellow, shone timidly through the blues and the greens and the reds of the church windows. Reckless motes of dust floated in a shaft of sunlight from the gap that the saint had left behind him, warming Michael's ankles and that strange, silent, red-raw part of him inside. Michael said: "So you're in it, too?"

"Oh, yes, I'm in it," said the young man. He was very thin and sharp-faced, and he wore a dark sort of gown, which made Michael wonder if he was in the choir.

"Have you been in it for a long time?"

"Well, that depends on what you call *long*. I've been in it a lot longer than you, Michael, but there are those who've been in it almost since the beginning of time."

Michael leaned forward, thought: *Without time or place*. Then he said, "How much do you know about me, exactly?"

"Quite a lot. I watch, you see."

"You—watch?" Michael echoed.

"Only, you might say I'm out of action, at the moment," continued the young man, smiling to himself. He took a long, green, leafy stem from a pocket in his gown. "Smell," he said, holding it out.

"Mmm," sighed Michael, closing his eyes.

"You don't have this in your world. The air's too thick."

"Who *are* you?" said Michael.

"That's beside the point," said the young man firmly,

twirling the stem in his fingers. "But I do have something to say to you, Michael. You've been through quite a lot, since you let us in, and we're quite aware that it hasn't been easy for you. What we want to do is make a little hole for you. You see, Michael, this is a sort of turning point. If you want out, just say so. But say so now, because from here on it gets steeper."

Michael blinked. "Steeper?" he repeated.

"I'm afraid so. How can I explain? Let's say, we're all working on a joint project. It's complicated, and there are many of us involved. Your Sparrow's the key man—he's bearing the brunt of it—and he's the only one in direct contact with HQ. But the mission is ours—all of ours—and yours, too, of course, if you decide to stay in. The point is, though, Michael, that your probationary period is over. You can stay with us, or not, as you wish. But if you want to go on helping, you'll have to be prepared to help in a slightly different way."

Michael squinted up at him. "How d'you mean?" he asked cautiously.

The young man sighed. "You know," he said, "that you've been helping us through your sympathy?"

"The Sparrow told me that," said Michael, "only, I—"

"You don't understand, I suppose. It's always like that at the beginning. You can't understand how a feeling that comes quite naturally can have such power. Just believe me that it does. Like many things, it is rare in its pure form, Michael, and rare elements often have amazing properties. Look at uranium!" He smiled mischievously.

Michael sighed, only a little enlightened.

"But as I told you," continued the young man, "we need to ask you to give us something more now. Take the next step, if you like. I should warn you—it's a big one." He waited, but Michael said nothing. "From now on," he continued, "you must be prepared to go further than sympathy."

"Further than . . ." stammered Michael, confused. "But . . ."

"Have you heard the word 'empathy,' my young friend?" asked the man in the gown softly.

"Well, yes, I . . ."

"It's a rare quality—far more rare and precious than the sympathy you've so freely, so easily, I might say, given."

Easily, thought Michael.

"And as it is more rare, so it is more powerful, and—" he looked Michael straight in the eye, "and it hurts the person who gives it, Michael. Hurts and changes him . . . or her," he added thoughtfully.

"Like a sacrifice," murmured Michael, thinking of Simon.

The young man looked at him in silence for a moment. "You're learning fast, Michael," he said at last and smiled.

Michael tried desperately to pull himself together. "Look," he said, "can I ask you some questions about all this?"

"Well, you can try," said the young man.

"I've got two questions," said Michael.

"Go ahead."

"Well, firstly, why couldn't the Sparrow've told me all this?"

The young man gazed thoughtfully over Michael's head.

"Actually," he said, "we didn't think he was the right

man to do it. We know you like him, and all that, but the fact is, there's no real reason why you should trust him. You know nothing about him for sure—and we happen to know that certain—er—doubts about his chances of success—"

"That person in the Principal's office . . ."

"Yes, that's what I mean. Nasty bit of work, that."

Michael smiled a little sadly. It seemed rather unreal to him, now.

"Whereas," resumed the young man, with another of his angular smiles, "we knew you'd be able to take my word for it."

"Because I've known you for years?" said Michael.

"Yes," said the young man simply. "Next question?"

Michael smiled, defeated. "All right," he said. "It's just, couldn't you please tell me what *SEI* means?"

"No, I couldn't," said the young man. "But if you should happen to guess it—well, that's your business. And I will tell you this. *SEI* is not a word, Michael. It's initials."

Michael sat up.

"Oh—" he said.

"Now listen," said the young man quickly. "It's my turn. This must be difficult for you, I know, because you're only seeing about a hundredth of what's really going on. But now at least you know what They're like, and you've also met a few of us. You know which side you're on, and you must know by now that it's the right side. But as I said you must realize that however satisfying it is to be on the right side in the Secret War, it is also very dangerous, and this is your chance to get out, with honor. We can't promise you safety, you know, Michael," he added seriously.

Michael stood up suddenly and gazed away from him, over the choir stalls.

"How about it?" said the young man.

Michael had been warned. But he could think of only one thing—that even the worst bits were better than nothing at all. So he paused only briefly before saying, "Yes, of course. So long as you can use me."

And Sarah Jane Yardley, emerging at the top of the stairs, said, "I beg your pardon?"

At the time, it seemed like the worst thing that could have happened. Michael faltered.

"I—I'm sorry," he said, in a rush, "I was just talking to—er—" He turned, found that the young man had gone, and felt immediately a great swell of disappointment. "He must've gone," he finished lamely. "He's—er—very shy."

Sarah Jane looked at him through her sea-gray eyes.

"This balcony stinks of magic," she remarked calmly. "Can't you smell it?"

"I didn't—know you came to this church," said Michael quickly.

Sarah Jane smiled.

"We don't," she said. "We usually go to All Saints'. But Mum's in the hospital around the corner, you know, and we're going to visit her at nine. So we thought it'd be easier to pop in here." She paused and sniffed at the air, rather like Hamlet the cat when he smelled fish, thought Michael. "It's fading, now," she said.

"Yes—er—I'm sorry about your mother," said Michael. "How is she?"

"All right," said Sarah Jane. "What are you doing up here?" she added, frankly curious.

Michael choked on *none of your business* and said:

"I—I just came up to look at a window."

"Oh, really?" said Sarah Jane. "Which one?"

"Well, that's the problem," said Michael morosely. "It's gone. It used to be over there," he added, gesturing vaguely.

"This one, you mean?" said Sarah Jane, going over to look. "But there's nothing missing, is there?"

Michael, who was sick of her hints and her sea-gray eyes, wished she'd go away. He sighed, and slouched over to point it out.

"It's over—" he began.

But she was right. The obscure saint, with his saffron-glass hair, was tending his green-glass garden once more. Michael could have hugged her.

"Had you forgotten where it was?" she asked huskily, "or was it magic, after all?"

Michael just grinned.

———

In the kitchen of No. 4, Juliet beat cake mixture, while Mrs. Devine, on her knees, cleaned the oven. Michael burst in, went to the fridge, saying "Hiya!" in his best American accent, and added, as his grandmother and sister stared at one another, "There's nothing to—"

"We bought some fruit punch for you, yesterday," said Jilly, stunned. "Are you feeling all right, Mike?"

Michael, delighted with the fruit punch, nodded airily at her.

Mrs. Devine sat up on her heels. "Where've you been, anyway?"

"Mass," said Michael. "Aren't you going?"

"Not till this evening," said Jilly. "Michael, have you been taking those tablets?"

"What tablets?" said Michael. "Oh, *those*. I don't know. Probably."

"Michael, *honestly* . . ."

But Michael only grinned to himself and tickled Jilly on the way to the sink.

"I'm not ticklish!" she protested lamely.

"Michael," began Mrs. Devine.

But he was gone.

"Well," she said, gazing after him quizzically. "There's a change of mood for you. He must be growing up, I suppose."

Jilly rinsed the mixing bowl.

"That's funny," she said. "I thought he'd done that years ago."

A Hard Day's Night

ighth period Mondays was history, in the library. Michael, sitting in the stuffy, uncomfortable library classroom, gazed up at the clock and considered the enigmatic Sparrow. Until Mr. Bentley, a lay-teacher, said:

"Right, Year nine, you've got twenty minutes to get yourselves some books. Back in here by three-fifteen, thanks, and no rabbling. Off you go."

The class shuffled out to the shelves in a mild, Monday-afternoon stupor. Michael, in there among them, wondered what they were supposed to be looking for.

"The catalog, first, meathead," said Paul, pulling him over by the sweater. "Convicts, convicts—"

"Convicts," said Michael vaguely, thinking immediately of the Artful Dodger. He'd always wondered, actually, if he mightn't have reformed, and got married, and had kids, because then . . .This he suggested, in a muddled sort of way, to Paul.

But Paul just sighed. "Sometimes I wonder about you," he said, looking at Michael over the open CIV-DEP drawer. "How could the Artful Dodger have descendants in Australia if he never really existed? Dickens only transported him at the end because he didn't know how else to get rid of him, Peebles said."

"Well, he could've hanged him," said Michael, disconcerted. "He killed off Fagin, poor bugger." Besides, as he added to himself, the Artful Dodger *did* exist. All book characters existed, for Michael, in their own sort of way. "You don't know what I mean, anyway," he told Paul, which unaccountably reminded him of *SEI*. Then he looked up and caught sight of the dictionary shelf.

"Where're you going *now?*" Paul whined, abandoning the catalog.

"Want to look something up," said Michael. "Wait on."

And he pulled the great, rice-leaved *Oxford* off the shelf.

"Look, Michael, he'll be after us, in a minute. Couldn't you do it later?"

"No," said Michael. *Screen, strangle, swipe* . . . "You're not scared of him, are you?"

"Don't be so smart. It was *you* who ended up in the Principal's office last week—"

"Must you remind me?" said Michael morosely, scanning pages. "The proportion of dirty words in the English language is absolutely amazing," he added.

"It's your mind," said Paul. "What're you looking for, anyway?"

But Michael had found it. The dictionary, impartial, said:

sўm'path/ў, n. The state of sharing or tendency to share emotion, sensation, condition, etc. of another person or thing; mental participation in another's trouble; compassion . . .

"Hmm," said Michael.

"Well, you knew *that*, didn't you? What're you doing *now*?"

"Just a sec. Have to compare it with . . ." *Electric, elephant, elevate, emasculate* (see?) . . . oh, here it was:

ĕm'path/ў, n. (psych.) The power of projecting one's personality into (and so fully comprehending) the object of contemplation . . .

"*Oh*," said Michael. That did sound steeper. For a moment he felt a cold hand around his heart. Then he looked up to see Paul with one of those caught-in-the-act expressions on his face, and Bentley looming. But the teacher only said, "Oh, there you are, Devine. You're wanted at the office. Hurry up!" before bustling past.

And Michael, exchanging quick, pained glances with Paul, could only shrug to himself and tear out of the library.

The office, with its three typing, telephone-answering secretaries (otherwise known as the ancillary staff), was across the lawn and along the hall from the chapel. Michael, skidding across the grass, wondered whatever he could have done *now*. Until:

"Someone wanted me?" he said nervously to the lady at the desk.

"You're Michael Devine, are you? Yes, dear, someone on the phone for you. They wouldn't let us take a message . . .that's right, over there."

Michael sighed. Was *that* all? Probably just Gran, or someone.

"Hello," he said into the receiver.

There was a brief, crackly pause.

"Hello?" said Michael again, glancing up at the secretary.

"There is still time," said a voice suddenly. "Do not go into your room tonight, and you will not have to help. Do not help, and you will not have to deal with us. Because you won't get away with it if you do, Devine. Do you understand?"

Michael threw down the receiver.

"All right, dear?" said the secretary.

"They must've hung up," said Michael.

———

But even after that, the thought of avoiding the cellar room never crossed Michael's mind. And, that night, he met the Gray Man.

It was the cracked mirror, leering over the room, that Michael saw first as he came down the stairs. But there was a reflection in it, a reflection with a grayish glow. The Gray Man, hunched in a corner, gazed up at him.

"How now, my Helper?" he sighed. "Thou hast been long in coming."

"Wh-what d'you want?" said Michael.

The Gray Man smiled the ghost of a smile. "Fear not," he said. "I could not harm thee if I wanted it so. The power, my Helper, lies in thy hands."

"The power?" said Michael. He stood motionless, never having gotten past the doorway. "Wh-what do you mean?"

"I wish to enlist thy help," said the Gray Man, and his black eyes seemed to cloud. "A long, long time ago, I left something undone, and because of this there is a knot in the tapestry. But now at last the knot may be unraveled, and stitched over, and the tapestry made perfect. We have only one opportunity. If we let it pass, the mission will fail."

"The *mission*?" said Michael. "I—I don't understand. What did you do—sir?"

The Gray Man bent his head. "Say rather, what did I *not* do. I, too, was a Helper, once. But I failed in my task."

Michael walked into the room and shut the door. He suddenly felt rather sick.

"They were the murderers," said the Gray Man, softly, "but I killed her, too. Because I was afraid to help her. Think on it, sweet youth! I, a man, was afraid—and so she wandered in the forest. And froze to death."

A smoke-gray mist began to swirl into the room. Michael swatted at it.

"Wh-where are you?" he faltered.

"Nowhere," said the Gray Man, a shape around which the mist writhed and blew. "I live in eternal twilight. Unless another Helper unravels the knot, I will be held in this thrall forever. If you want to help, you must enter in."

"What?"

"The scene, sweet youth, must be replayed. You must come in to me and do what I did not."

"But—but you can't change history—"

"Oh, yes, you can," said the Gray Man, reaching forward with his fingertips. "Touch me, Helper."

For a moment, he was perfectly distinct, stretching out with his gray fingers. Michael swallowed, thrust out his arm, and felt a sudden and blinding coldness, as if he had plunged into icy water.

The night was dark and bitterly cold. The Helper, shutting the door quietly behind him, suddenly felt stone at his fingertips, and looked up to find that he was leaving, not a house, but the bleak gray of a cobbled tower. It didn't seem strange. The Helper stepped briskly into the night.

Snow crunched, like frozen sand, beneath his feet. Up ahead, as promised, stood the horse, dappled gray and blowing smoke. The boy stood beside it, holding the reins. He grinned, starry-eyed, and handed them over.

The Helper mounted and sat, very high and tense, on the dappled-gray back.

"Good luck, sir," said the boy. "I shan't tell a soul."

"Loyal friend," said the Helper. "God grant I may see you again."

The boy stood on tiptoe, kissed his hand, and ran away without another word. Left alone, the Helper sighed, felt the animal beneath him stir restlessly. He looked anxiously around him, pulled the black flowing cloak over his shoulders, and signaled sharply to the horse with the heel of his black riding boot. The horse moved off into the night.

The Helper saw moonlight on snow, watched the shadows of the trees that dappled about him, and felt a bright, chill breeze as the air pushed past and made his cloak fly out like wings behind him. With his head down close to the horse's neck, he smelled leather and sweat, and became one with the animal beneath him.

The snow sang with stillness. It was painfully pure. As was the girl, wrapped in green velvet, standing alone in a clearing.

The Helper drew the reins in, cantered, then trotted

around the space inside the trees. The horse snorted smoke and shook his soft gray mane. And the Helper, dark and slight, slid out of the saddle and stood holding the warm, damp head.

"I have come," he whispered, "to help."

The girl gazed out of her green velvet cloak. She was trembling.

"I-it's s-so c-c-cold—" she managed, with an effort. "I—thought you would n-never c-c-come—"

And all at once, the Helper understood that the Gray Man never did. The story was taking a turn for the better, the second time. He had only to take her arm, and . . . The Helper glanced nervously around, just in time to see four men emerge simultaneously from the trees.

It began to snow, very lightly, into the blue and white silence. The Helper, with the reins in one hand and the girl's elbow in the other, stood still.

Run said a cold voice in his head. *This is not your fight. Save yourself.*

But the Helper stood his ground. He put the girl behind him and drew his sword. It glinted in the moonlight. The men began to close on them, and then . . .

Then halted. Stared. Dropped their swords. And ran.

The Helper stood motionless in the snow. Then, on impulse, he looked down at himself and understood.

For his body was in an odd state of change. The black cloak and boots were fading, fading, and other garments were thickening from beneath to take their place. At the same time, he felt something go out of him, in a rush, through his fingertips. Suddenly, he found himself shivering in a familiar black duffle coat and jeans.

He turned, confused, to the girl. Her green velvet cloak

89

had disappeared, leaving her standing, incongruous in jeans and a navy blue coat, over which streamed a mass of long, dark hair . . .

"*SEI*," said Sarah Jane.

"What're *you* doing here?" said Michael.

"Shhh!"—pointing—

For on the gray-dappled horse, a man and a green-cloaked girl rode off into the silent snow.

"They're gone," said Michael hollowly, peering into the white distance. Then he turned and stared at her. "What *are* you doing here?" he repeated.

"What a silly question," remarked Sarah Jane, shaking snow out of her hair.

Michael nodded tiredly at her.

"So it is," he sighed. "How long've *you* been in it, then?"

Sarah Jane looked at him through her sea-gray eyes.

"I think I've always been in it," she said, after a moment. "Haven't you?"

Michael, blinking at her, said: "Yes, I suppose I have."

The Sparrow, leaning in his dark suit against a tree trunk, said dryly: "I hope you two are having fun."

They both recoiled, as if he'd struck them. He looked at them, his image wavered a little, and his expression grew gentler.

"I'm sorry," he said. "I frightened you again."

"Why are you angry with us?" said Sarah Jane.

"I am not angry with you, Yardley. It's just—it's just that you don't understand." He smiled a little sadly at them, and Michael saw by the way he was holding his arm that the wound had not healed. "You change history," said the Sparrow, "as if it were—"

"Easy?" said Sarah Jane.

Sea and steely grays met. The Sparrow let it pass.

"I have a difficult night ahead of me," he said to Michael. "I may need your help, come the morning, Devine. There will be—retributions—"

"For what we've done?" cried Sarah Jane.

"It's not your fault," said the Sparrow, quickly. "You must not blame yourselves, whatever happens. You did only what you were asked to do." After a pause he continued more slowly. "You see, you *can* change history. But you can't always get away with it." He looked at them thoughtfully. "I'm going to send you back now," he said. "But I won't be very accurate, tonight, I'm afraid. I must save my strength. And so you will have to get yourselves home the best way you can."

"Of course," said Sarah Jane apologetically, and the Sparrow, with a sudden movement, patted her dark head as if stroking a kitten. Then, looking up, he saw that Michael was pale and shivering in the moonlight. The Sparrow leaned forward, and for a moment, to Michael, his image seemed to have stopped flickering altogether. He was solid, firm, and reassuring.

"Devine," he said. "Sympathy is sympathy. But empathy *hurts*." He laid a hand on the boy's arm.

Then, with a flutter and sigh, he was gone.

———

There was a brief, bubbling sort of journey—like jumping into deep water—and, suddenly, they were there. *But where?* Michael thought, peering into the much warmer darkness around him. There was a sort of step, behind him, and so he sat down on it.

"Wh-where are we?" said Sarah Jane.

"I'm not sure," said Michael.

But then, just as he noticed that the step beneath him was damp, something clicked. He got up quickly.

"What is it?"

"Step's damp. Listen, there's nothing to worry about. I know exactly where we are—"

"Where?"

Michael turned nervously, peered into the dark alley behind them. "That's Selby Lane," he said.

Sarah Jane squinted at it. "D'you mean we're in Coleridge?" she said.

"Yes, of course. Where d'you live?"

"Coleridge Heights."

Michael's heart sank. "Oh, no," he said.

For it was pitch-dark, and Coleridge Heights was a long way away. Michael fought with his watch. "Can you see?"

"It says two-fifteen," said Sarah flatly.

"No buses, then."

"Taxis?"

For a moment, Michael's face lit up. Then he said, "Money . . ."

They pawed through their pockets. Michael found a bus ticket, a stick of chewing gum, a crumpled tissue, a button, and three silver coins. Sarah Jane had a bobby pin, a small comb, a handkerchief, a supermarket receipt, a dollar, and two silver coins. They looked at each other nervously.

"It's not nearly enough," said Michael, at last. "Not for Coleridge Heights."

"We could ask him to wait and get the money from home . . ."

"Yes," said Michael, "but if you're going to do something like that, you may as well call your parents right away and save yourself the trouble. You'd be sure to wake up someone."

"But—but—"

"Boy, are we ever going to get it," said Michael wryly. "Don't cry," he added.

"I'm not," said Sarah Jane.

There didn't seem much point arguing with her. In a brief silence, footsteps echoed up toward them and off down the street. It was so very dark.

"Look," said Michael suddenly. "I mean, listen. I've just—oh, *why* didn't I think of it before? Don't worry, we're all right—we've just got to find a phone."

"What're you going to do?"

Michael grabbed her hand and pulled her off down the lane.

"It's okay. I've just thought of someone I can call."

"B-but what'll they *say*?"

Michael grinned into the darkness.

"That's just it. He won't mind. He knows."

"He *knows*?" said Sarah Jane. "You mean, you've *told* someone?"

"And it's a ruddy good thing I did, too. The only thing is, he hasn't got a car. But he can use ours. He *can* drive—"

Sarah Jane stopped dead. Michael tripped.

"What the—?"

Footsteps. A figure in the mouth of the alley. And whispers.

Michael squeezed her hand and pulled her slowly into the protection of the shadows. The footsteps paused, continued slowly down the lane, quickened, paused again, became faint, and ceased altogether. Michael waited. Then he pulled Sarah Jane swiftly through the shadows.

"Not far," he whispered. "It's the post office I'm after. It's over the road." They came out suddenly into the open darkness of the main street. "It shouldn't be so bad here, anyway," he said.

And bit his lip.

For there were noises, strange noises behind them. Noises like a cross between a door creaking and the wail of an electric piano. They echoed, ricocheted back and forth across the street. Michael felt his fists clench in his pockets.

"Where's it coming from?" whispered Sarah Jane. "What *is* it!"

"I don't know. If we could just get across . . ."

A car swished past them, and they ducked back quickly to avoid the light. But a car was normal; the headlights, passing on up the road, made them feel better. Michael said, "Come on."

They ran across the street. On the other side, the noises seemed fainter.

The wooden telephone cubicles, lined up on either side of the dark passage that was the entrance to the post office, were well lit. Pulling out change, they ducked into the first one.

"Damn," Michael hissed. "It's dead."

But Sarah, dainty and pale under the fluorescent light, just popped into the next one. After all, there were eight. "It's all right!" she hissed. "This one works."

Michael fumbled with the coin slot, glanced confusedly at the instructions, dialed the number, and: RRRing-RRRing silence, said the receiver. RRRing-RRRing silence. RRRing-RRRing silence.

They waited, staring at each other, each seeing a pale

face with wide, darkened eyes, ghostly in the harsh light. While the screeching, wailing noises, bouncing across the street and back again, became louder. And louder. And . . .

"Hello?" said a froggy voice in the receiver.

But Michael was shaking so hard that he could barely grip the phone. He opened his mouth and found, as if in a nightmare, that he was unable to get the words out.

"Hello?" said Simon's froggy voice again. "Hello?"

"D-don't h-hang up," Michael gasped into the receiver. "S-Simon—"

"*Michael*," said Simon. His voice seemed to spring to life. "Where are you?"

"P-post office. P-please will you come and—"

"In the main street, you mean? Hang on, Michael, I'm coming straight away, all right? See you." The receiver clicked. Michael, gripping the side of the cubicle, tried hard to get hold of himself.

"He's c-coming," he said.

But Sarah Jane didn't hear him. She was at the door of the box, peering into the street.

"F-faces," she said gripping his coat. "I saw f-faces, in the street—"

"You *didn't*," said Michael furiously.

"D-did. F-faces. Horrible—" She shuddered.

"Look," he said, in a voice that hardly seemed his own, "we're all right. Simon's coming to get us. You're just panicking . . ."

But her grip on the coat only tightened, and she pointed out into the street. Michael felt as if he'd swallowed his own stomach. There *were* faces.

And the noises were moving, very slowly, up the street.

The ricochet effect seemed less pronounced. They were congregating—and approaching.

Michael prayed. Two cars swished past. The phones gazed impassively at them. Sarah Jane shook. And Michael held on to the tail of her coat.

Then, faces, noises. For a moment, they seemed passing, passing, past—but, no—there was a jingling, a soft tread coming up the dark passage toward them . . .

Sarah Jane shrieked.

And Simon, in pajamas, with the moth-eaten sweater thrown over the top, jingling a bunch of keys on his finger, turned quite white.

Michael often thought, later, about the half-hour or so that followed. It was odd, to say the least, because all the while he was only three-quarters conscious. He would get snatches of conversation, here and there, which confused him further—and every so often he would feel himself washed over by the most vivid impressions. Like the interior of his grandmother's car, going round and round and round . . .

And then there was Sarah Jane, sitting in the front next to Simon, trying to tell him through a spasmodic sort of sobbing where she lived.

"Michael?" said Simon softly, opening the car door. "Come on, mate, we're home."

Michael tried to focus on him, failed, but managed to crawl out of the car. Then, suddenly, there was the sound of a key in a lock.

"That's right, mate, come on in. Nope, on the thing, here. Oh, all right, on the floor, then . . ."

Michael, lying on Simon's floor, with Simon's rug over him, was out like a light.

Ducks and Drakes

Michael awoke the next morning in a state of confusion. Beneath him was a brown linoleum floor, around him was a tatty sort of rug, and in his nostrils was a bracing scent of turpentine. He caught a sleepy breath and sat up quickly.

"Oh, good," said Simon, hair (with green paint in it) on end. "I was just about to wake you. You wouldn't want your gran to catch you in here. Sometimes she comes down quite early."

Michael, leaning on his elbow, squinted up at him. "Hi," he said.

Simon grinned. "Yes," he said. "Well, I'm afraid I had to wake her, last night."

"For the keys?" said Michael, through the husk of his early-morning voice. "Gee whiz, I never thought of that."

"Hmm. It was all right, really. She was very nice."

"Yes, but I wonder what she *thought*."

"Well, she'd hardly suspect you, old chap. At least we've diverted suspicion."

Michael bit his lip. "Look, Simon, I'm dreadfully sorry about last night. I know you don't just go around phoning people at two o'clock in the morning. But we were desperate."

Simon, sitting on the table, frowned. "Don't be idiotic," he said. "You don't start worrying about manners when you think you're in trouble."

Michael thought he had a point there. He shivered, and said softly, "All those noises. And the f-faces. I don't know who—what—was after us, but . . ." He faded out, rubbing his eyes. He had just noticed that he felt like death warmed over.

Simon continued to frown at him, looking very much more worried than usual. "Who was the girl?" he asked, at last.

"Oh, golly, I don't know," sighed Michael. "I mean, I do, but I haven't the slightest idea about why she turned up all of a sudden. Believe it or not, she's a second former at Jilly's school."

"The convent, you mean?"

Michael nodded. "Jilly's her class prefect. I only met her last Thursday. She came to tea—Jilly's coaching her French, you know. I guess—I guess I was watching her, if you know what I mean—but I didn't know she had anything to do with the War . . ."

"The War?" said Simon, confused. "What d'you mean, the War?"

Michael bit his lip, and looked up dubiously. He said, "I guess you're in it, now, whether you like it or not."

For it *was* a Secret War, thought Michael to himself, but did that mean the War was a secret? He had never been asked not to tell anyone—and if Simon hadn't known something about it he wouldn't have been able to help . . .

"Well," he said, "you're obviously not one of Them—"

"Look," said Simon, "don't tell me. I've forgotten already."

But Michael had already decided. "It's all right," he said. "I can't see why I shouldn't tell you what I think." He got up stiffly and walked over to the window.

"You *have* lost weight," Simon remarked, looking at him.

"Look, don't *you* start," said Michael impatiently. "Just listen, all right?"

"Go on," said Simon.

"Well, let's say, I'm sort of involved in this—er—thing. Call it a job. And let's say, while I'm on the job, all these strange—er—things keep happening to me. Say I'm helping someone who knows an awful lot more about it than me. Right?"

"Okay," said Simon.

"Well, when I first came in, I thought it was more or less MI5 stuff—you know, James Bond and all that. Only not so silly. After all, what spies go on with—that's a Secret War, isn't it?"

Simon frowned more deeply. "A Secret War?" he repeated.

"When I found out there was magic in it," Michael continued softly, "I just sort of extended the idea. You know—spy stuff, except with magic tricks. James Bond as a wizard, if you know what I mean."

Simon tried to imagine Bond with a big pointy hat on, and failed. This was *not* his idea of magic.

"Michael . . ." he said worriedly. But Michael was working something out.

"That was all wrong, too," he said, "or at least, not anywhere near the full story. Because it's more than just magic. It's—it's people from different times—and ghosts, and saints—and even—well, different forms of life, from different worlds. And you seem to be able to just bump into them or even cross over into different times yourself. So it isn't just like somebody waving a magic wand. But now I know what it is—what it's all about."

Simon blinked.

"It's easy; it's simple," said Michael. "It's about reality."

"*Reality?*" said Simon.

Michael glanced at him.

"Gee, Simon," he said. "I didn't think anything would surprise you."

Simon just looked at him. "Go on," he said, after a moment.

"Well," Michael resumed carefully, "what would you say if I told you I thought reality had layers in it?"

Simon smiled, slightly. "I think I'm beginning to understand."

"Are you?" said Michael, relieved. "Well, listen, here's what I think. The world's sort of like a building—a high rise—with stories. Things are going on on every level. See? Right now we're sitting on one level, and—and the War's, say, just below us. But there're holes, in the floor. People can climb up to me—and I can fall through to them—just when I least expect it."

Simon frowned at him.

"Oh."

Michael paused. "D'you still think I'm sane?" he asked hesitantly.

"Well," said Simon, "you're certainly *logical*."

Michael grinned at him. But he was beginning to wonder, all the same, where it would all end. And there was still *SEI* to worry about.

———

But it was Tuesday morning, after all, and despite last

night's events Michael had somehow to drag himself to school. It was already seven when he nicked furtively out of No. 1, and he would have bolted straight down to his room had not something begun to niggle at him at the top of the stairs.

Michael paused. He was conscious of a tight, asthmatic sort of feeling; a fear very faint and very difficult to define. He could only assume, with some disquiet, that there was another visitor in his room.

When he got downstairs, however, the feeling seemed to fade. The room was as he had left it, last night. So he put his discomfort down to nerves, and began to change his clothes.

Jeans were swapped for trousers, blue shirt for white, and the gray, V-necked school sweater was pulled anyhow over the top. Michael, catching sight of himself in the cracked mirror, agreed in a distracted sort of way that he *was* looking thin, and wished, as he often did, that he was the Invisible Man. Then he moved in closer, and peered through the crack at his face.

It was his eyes you noticed first. They were round and very brown, shadowed underneath, as though the skin was bruised. He had a freckled, snub nose and hollow cheeks—a strange combination. Michael, looking at himself properly for the first time since the mirror cracked, thought with surprise that he had changed. In fact, meeting his own eyes in the glass gave him quite a fright. So he glanced away.

But it was no use. The feeling was still there.

Was it—a noise? Or was it only in his head? It wasn't in the room; in fact, it seemed closer than that. And, for a very unnerving moment, Michael thought he was making it himself. Then it seemed to him it was a voice;

that something was calling, from inside his head. For *that* was what it felt like.

And *that* was what it was.

But what could he do? What was it trying to tell him? Distressed, he glanced again around the room. Then he noticed something. On his dressing table, at the base of the crack, was a small china figurine—in the shape of a sparrow.

Suddenly he knew exactly what to do. He picked up the figurine, raised his arm, and sent it smashing to the floor.

For a moment Michael stared, aghast, at the fragments, without the faintest idea what had possessed him—but then abruptly, the broken china vanished. And he looked up to see the Sparrow standing before him.

Michael opened his mouth to scream, but one look from the Sparrow stilled him.

"Wh-what happened?" he demanded.

The Sparrow said faintly, "Do you mind if I—" and sat down quickly on the bed.

"Is—is there anything I can get you?" said Michael.

But the Sparrow, with his arm resting limply by his side, only shook his head. Michael looked at him worriedly.

"Was—was it my fault?" he asked.

The Sparrow closed his eyes. "No," he sighed. "I said there would be retributions. Use your imagination, Devine."

"Them," said Michael.

"Yes, Devine. That was—how do you call it?—a close shave. They almost had me that time. And next time, it will take less."

"*Less?*" said Michael. "But . . ."

The Sparrow looked up sharply. "Don't worry about me, Devine. Just worry about the mission. I still have time, and that's all that matters."

But it wasn't. The Sparrow mattered, all right. Michael opened his mouth to protest, but then caught the steely-gray gaze and was silent.

"You've saved my life," said the Sparrow, without emotion. "Now, Devine, they'll really be after you."

Michael smiled.

"They're after me already," he said.

Michael found his family in the kitchen, just sitting down to breakfast. This was unfortunate, so far as he was concerned, because it meant he had to eat something. He sighed and sat down bravely at the table.

"Take a multivitamin, Mikey," said Robyn. "You may need it."

Michael started.

"Wh-what—?" he began.

"We've got a story for you," said Mrs. Devine, laughing, "that's all. Who d'you think was on our doorstep at two o'clock this morning?"

Michael almost dropped the milk bottle.

"Careful!" said Jilly.

"Who?" said Michael.

"Simon Collins," said Mrs. Devine. "And it gave me quite a shock, I can tell you. You know what a heavy sleeper I am—well, I was dead to the world—"

"And I heard this knocking," said Robyn. "I was terrified. I thought it was a burglar—"

"Burglars don't *knock*," Michael snapped.

"So she came in and woke me up—"

"That took about half an hour," said Robyn.

" . . . and I didn't want to open the door, very much, either—"

"So I was round the corner," said Robyn, "with a frying pan, to whop 'im one—"

"But I had the chain on," said Mrs. Devine, "and so I just took a peek—"

"And it was only Simon," said Robyn, still disappointed.

"So what did he want?" said Michael hoarsely.

"The car keys, of all things. At two o'clock in the morning! He's certainly never done anything like that before . . ."

"I hope he doesn't make a habit of it," said Michael.

"He's probably got a girlfriend," said Robyn airily.

"Oh, how would you know?" Michael snapped. "Besides, who the hell would have the cheek to go and see his girlfriend at two o'clock in the morning *in somebody else's car*? Honestly, Robyn, you're the limit."

"Just settle down, Michael," said Mrs. Devine. "I won't have you swearing at the table. Anyway, Robyn, it was an emergency. He said that much. And he was still in pajamas, so it must've taken him by surprise. I would've liked to ask him, but he was in too much of a hurry."

"Besides," said Jilly, "that wouldn't have been very polite, Gran."

"No," said Mrs. Devine, "I don't like to pry."

And a good thing, too, thought Michael. He wished someone would change the subject. He didn't feel up to it, himself. One thing, though, was certain: suspicion, as Simon had said, was successfully diverted. Mission accomplished, thought Michael—and then, as he considered the other mission, felt rather sick.

"D'you know," said Robyn obligingly, "it's four days since we put that ad in the paper."

"Well," smiled Jilly, "looks like you're safe, Rob."

"I'd better leave it in, though, I think," said Mrs. Devine. "Just till the end of the week. That seems fair."

Robyn grimaced. "Anyway," she said, getting up, "I've got to go. We've got a practice at eight-thirty."

"You'll be overrehearsed before you're finished," said Jilly with disapproval.

"We've only got a week," Robyn protested. She pecked her grandmother on the cheek, plucked her school case from the hall, and was gone, clattering down the stairs.

With an effort, Michael swallowed porridge. He glanced at Jilly and said casually: "Sarah Jane be in this week?"

"Don't think so," said Jilly. "She's a bit tied up with visiting her mother. I told you about that, didn't I?"

"Er—yes," said Michael. "Yes, I think you did."

He frowned to himself. So she wouldn't be in this week. But he had to see her, for now they were partners in crime, as it were.

"Will you see her today?" said Michael.

"I see her every morning, when I do the roll," said Jilly.

"Oh."

But there was nothing he could tell her, not through Jilly. And anyway, she might very well take the day off, after last night. That, thought Michael with a yawn, would've been the sensible thing to do. Still, they would have to meet somewhere; he would have to call. And no one in the family was to know about it. He would not stand for any kindly, amused interest from his grandmother and Jilly, any "Mickey's got a girlfriend" from Robyn—that would be the bitter end. Besides, it wasn't *that*, at all, was it? Michael quickly avoided the thought, and wondered how many Yardleys there were in the phone book.

He really did wonder, as he was crossing Darley Road, why he was going to school that day. He still felt like death warmed up. But then, he supposed, it was always best to lie low. Staying in bed was a bit too obvious, anyway, and his cellar room no safe house.

So he walked on determinedly toward the bus stop until, by the road, he saw an old lady. At first he didn't really understand why he was taking any notice of her— but he was. And as he drew closer, she began to look a little sinister. She looked at him, and said: "Excuse me, young man . . ."

Michael faltered. He was only three and a half houses from the bus stop, where a group of St. John's boys rabbled gleefully. He glanced nervously at them, hoped fervently that nothing strange would happen, and went over to her.

She smiled at him with glossy plastic teeth and looked right through him with colorless eyes. "Could you tell me the way to Selby Lane?" she said.

Now he really smelled a rat. But there was nothing he could do. He said nervously, "Of course. You—er—go down this road, then turn left. Then you walk along the main street, and it's just about halfway down." Trying to get rid of her, he pointed down the road. "Er—the main street's just down there," he said.

But Michael should never have raised his arm like that. It seemed to set in motion a most undesirable chain of events. For, as he pointed, a large black bird landed on his arm.

Michael froze.

The bird, gazing at him with a bright yellow eye, dug its claws into his flesh. It dropped something white and crumpled from its beak. Then, with a push that made Michael stumble backward, it took off. And disappeared.

The old lady was nowhere to be seen. But the paper, creased and dusty, lay at his feet. Michael bit his lip, knelt, and picked it up.

YOU WILL NOT ALWAYS BE ABLE TO HIDE BEHIND THE SPARROW. THIS IS YOUR LAST CHANCE. STOP HELPING, OR WE START ON YOUR HOUSE.

Michael crushed the note into a ball and shoved it into his pocket. The mob at the bus stop were happily unconscious of anything unusual. Michael approached them.

"Where'd you spring from?" asked Paul, as they lined up to board the bus. "You're late," he added, eyeing him quizzically.

But Michael, biting his lip, was silent.

———

All the same, nothing happened at school that day, and Michael, walking home in bright afternoon sunlight, had the ominous feeling that this was the calm before the storm.

The flat, sunny and serene, offered him no answers. Michael dumped his schoolbag on the settee, felt an unexpected craving for a carrot, and went to get one out of the fridge. Then he lay down quietly in the patches of latticed sun on the living room floor. And thought about *SEI.*

"Michael, is that you?" called a voice from the attic.

"Is *what* me?" said Michael.

"Oh, very funny. If you want the truth, I can hear you eating."

"Well," said Michael, going up, "it *was* a carrot."

"Oh," said Jilly, "that's healthy of you. How was school?"

She was sitting at her desk, with an open math book before her and Hamlet on her lap. Michael, seeing a new acquisition on the bed, said: "*Colditz,* now, eh? Will it never end?"

"Probably not," replied Jilly carelessly. "I said, 'How was school?' "

Michael sighed. "All right," he said. At least they weren't taking that much notice of him. Michael had decided to be neurotic only when he could do it inconspicuously. It was hard, though, with things like that bird turning up at odd moments . . .

"Er—sorry?"

"I said, did you know Simon's going to paint the halls for us? He needs the money, of course, and Gran said we need the paint job."

Michael felt his mouth twitch.

"Back-scratching, hey?" he said. "Whatever happened to the white ants, anyway?"

"Oh, I don't know. I suppose Gran left it to him. He's really very handy, isn't he, considering he's an artist?"

"He can do anything," said Michael fervently.

"But he hasn't said anything about last night. Except he paid Gran for the gas." And she paused, lightly tapping her book with the blunt end of a pencil. "He's an interesting sort of person," she said hesitantly, after a moment.

Michael laughed.

"What's so funny?"

"Well, it's not, really," said Michael, suddenly sick of playing ducks and drakes. "It's just I know you've got a crush on him."

Taken by surprise, Jilly turned a confused shade of pink.

"Well," said Michael, annoyed. "You have. For at least six months."

"He's only been here six months," Jilly snapped.

"Now you're angry," sighed Michael.

"I'm not!" said Jilly, angrily.

"You are so. And I must say, I don't ruddy-well see why."

"I wish you'd leave me alone," said Jilly, flicking furiously through her textbook.

But at that point there was a faint noise in the attic's low roof. A sort of scuttling. Michael started. "What's that?" he hissed.

"What's what?" said Jilly, looking up in surprise.

"Can't you hear it?" said Michael, peering upward. He paused, listening. *"There,"* he said. "There, again—"

"Probably pigeons," said Jilly, forgetting to be cross. "Sometimes, at night—"

But Michael gazing fearfully at the ceiling, found it difficult to get hold of himself. The noise reminded him of last night.

"Th-there's something up there," he said unsteadily.

"Michael, you're trembling."

"I'm not—"

"Look," said Jilly, "it is only a noise, really—I've often heard it before."

"Yes," said Michael, closing his eyes. "Only a noise."

"Michael, what's wrong? Can't you tell me?"

Michael looked up at her. "No," he said, shaking his head. "No." The noise faded, and with it went the panic. Michael began to feel deeply ashamed of himself. Pigeons. *Honestly.*

Jilly sighed, and made a few marks on her exercise book. "You're not really in this family, you know," she said.

"So, what's new?" said Michael gloomily. He stuck his hands in his pockets and trailed off down the stairs, rolling the crumpled-up note between his fingers.

Partners in Crime

It should have been sacrilegious, Michael thought, for Robyn to wear it like that. Standing on the table, in the living room, with her grandmother sticking pins in the hem. Quite bizarre, really, when you thought about it. But then, the dress seemed somehow above all that. And what Robyn didn't know wouldn't hurt her. He hoped. All the same . . .

"*Ouch!*" squeaked Robyn.

"Talk about a crybaby," mumbled Mrs. Devine, through the pins she gripped in her mouth.

"That's crooked," Michael warned.

And Jilly, coming lightly down the stairs, said: "I wish you wouldn't do that, Gran. What if you swallowed one?"

Michael chuckled to himself and leafed idly through the script. "Go on, then," he said.

"You have to give me the bit before it," said Robyn.

Michael ran his eyes down the page. "Er—*But, Princess, what can we do?*— is that it?"

"Do it properly," said Robyn.

"Look, Sunshine, you're lucky I'm doing it at all." But he sighed, and read with as much expression as he could reasonably muster: "*But, Princess, what can we do? Your wicked father has banished me from the kingdom—I*

111

daren't show my face at his court, let alone request your precious hand. And I must be gone, at midnight."

Robyn sighed, and clasped her hands. *"Oh, my dear Prince! What if I never see you again?"*

"It must not come to that," read Michael. *"I must take you away."*

"Take me away? But—but the guards! My father! The witch!"

"I do not fear them."

"Well, I do."

Jilly giggled. "You ought to watch that line," she said. "You'll end up getting a laugh."

Michael read on, silently. "That teacher of yours must be crackers," he said, after a moment. "What little brat's going to say a line like that?"

"Like what?"

"Like *Oh, Princess, how I adore you.*"

"Yes," said Robyn, "well, we cut that bit, anyway."

"Sensitive woman."

"Don't be mean, Mikey."

"Well, look," said Michael, "could we have a look at something you're actually performing?"

"All right," said Robyn, agreeably. "Let's do the beginning, then."

Michael flicked through the stenciled sheets.

"Not all this bit with the Narrator?"

"Robyn, will you stand up *straight*," mumbled Mrs. Devine, through her pins. "You'd be the first to complain if it was crooked, my dear—"

"Look, Gran, let me hold the pins for you, for goodness' sake," said Jilly, coming over.

Michael sighed.

"Far, far away in a land beyond the morning star,

was a kingdom, ruled by a wicked wizard. And this wicked wizard had a beautiful daughter, whom he kept locked up in a tower. She was very unhappy. Until, one day, as she was crying in her room, something happened . . ."

"*Oh,*" sobbed the Princess, suddenly standing there on the table before him. "*I—I am so unhappy!*"

Michael sat up. "Robyn," he said sharply, "how d'you do that?"

"D-do what?" said Robyn, still with a sob in her voice.

"Say it, like that. Like the Princess would."

"Oh," said Robyn, suddenly understanding him. "It's easy. I just melt."

"*Melt?*"

"You know, melt into her."

"Who, the Princess?"

"Yes, of course. Who else?"

Michael forgot there was anyone else in the room. He said carefully, "D'you mean, you stop being yourself?"

"No," said Robyn. "I mean, I just start being someone else."

Michael stared at her. It was like a revelation; it hit him in the chest. Identity, the Sparrow had said. A war across identity. A war across time, and place, and even . . . identity.

"Michael, go on," said Robyn impatiently.

"Oh," said Michael, hoarsely. "All right." The more I know, he thought, the more I don't know. He stored it away, for later.

———

After that, he really *had* to talk to Sarah Jane.

It was on the Wednesday, just over a week after the

mirror cracked, that Michael had his chance. He had a real bit of luck, that morning. The girls had left early, for a rehearsal before school, and even his grandmother was out of the flat by eight. As this was because of a dental appointment, it wasn't exactly luck for Gran, but . . .

But, thought Michael, pulling out the telephone directory, at least now he could call Sarah Jane in peace. Quickly he opened it toward the back and stumbled into W. He flicked past X, pounced on Y, ran his finger down the column. Yardstick. No, too far. He turned back a page and . . .

There were a few Yardleys, but only one at Coleridge Heights. Michael, cradling the phone book, picked up the receiver, then put it down again.

Who was he? He didn't want to be Michael Devine, for her father, because he might mention it to Mrs. Devine. And he didn't want *her* to know he'd called. Michael clutched the phone book, thought. A name, a name. Preferably one he wouldn't forget. And a story.

Michael made notes.

He was—the brother of a friend at school (*that* was true)—and—poor Mary had the measles—so he's calling to ask Sarah what she's been missing at school. His name is—how about—Peter Fanshawe?

All right, thought Michael, now dial the number. Go on, *dial* it . . .

"Hello?"

"Er—hello—could I speak to Sarah Jane, please?"

"Sarah who?"

Wrong number. Michael swore to himself, started all over again. The phone rang once. The phone rang twice. The phone rang . . .

114

"Hello?"

"Er—this is P-Peter F-Fanshawe—"

"Oh, hello, Michael."

"Look, you're not supposed to know who I am!"

"Well, never mind," said Sarah Jane. "Let's pretend the fairies told me. Did you go to school, yesterday?"

Michael sighed.

"Yes, I had to. I've been taking a few too many days off lately. I'm trying to be less conspicuous. Listen, I can't talk, I'm late. But I've got to see you."

"Oh, have you?" said Sarah Jane, velvet-voiced.

"Yes," said Michael quickly. "Just to talk. D'you think we could meet?"

"Well, we're both at school today," said Sarah Jane anxiously. "And this afternoon I have to go and visit Mum."

"Oh," said Michael.

There was a pause.

"Hello?" he said, after a moment.

"Yes, I'm here. I'm thinking. Listen, could you come to the hospital?"

"The hospital?" Michael repeated, surprised.

"Yes. Look, you don't have to worry. Dad's busy this afternoon, so I was going alone, anyway. I have to get a taxi up—"

"You're obsessed with taxis, aren't you?"

They both giggled. It was a very private sort of joke.

"If I got there at a quarter to four," said Sarah Jane, "we could talk for half an hour before I went in to see Mum. Could you come, d'you think?"

"I'll be there," said Michael. "Where shall I meet you?"

"D'you know the main entrance?"

"I can find it. Quarter to four, then?"

"All right," said Sarah Jane. "Listen, Michael, I—I'm glad you're in it, too . . ."

"Yes," said Michael, "well, that's why we've got to talk, isn't it?"

———

"The *hospital*?" said Paul. "What for?"

Michael had thought it would be easy. Some people actually got off at the hospital; he had only to stay on the bus. But he had forgotten that Paul himself often got off at the hospital and was already convinced he was cracking up. This, so far as Paul was concerned, was the last straw.

"I—er—have to meet someone."

"Yeah? Who?"

"Well, it's a girl, if you must know."

"A *girl*?" said Paul.

Michael colored, in spite of himself. "Look," he said, "it's no one you know, so just—"

"From Sancta Sophia?"

"Well—yes—"

"I bet I do, then. What form?"

"Second. Look, Paul—"

"You've been very shady about this, I must say."

"Will you dry *up*! It's not that sort of girl, anyway."

"Not *what* sort of girl? She a relation, or something?"

"Well, no—"

"Then what're you on about? Can I see her?"

Michael sighed. "Oh, all right," he said, "if she's there."

And she was, unfortunately, standing on the steps by the entrance. She saw them get off the bus and then pretended she hadn't. Michael gestured furtively.

"*Her?*" said Paul, peering into the grounds. "That's the new kid, Sarah Yardley, isn't it?"

"Sarah *Jane*," Michael growled.

"She's in my sister's class," said Paul.

"Yes, that's right. Jilly's the class prefect. Satisfied?"

Paul eyed him quizzically. "You're a funny one. All right, I'm going. Have fun."

Michael grunted at him, dumped his bag by the gate, and walked up toward the entrance. Sarah Jane smiled.

"Hello."

"Hello," said Michael, fighting a sudden desire to turn right around and walk back home again. "Is—er—everything all right?"

"Yes. I—er—yes."

Then, for a moment, they just grinned at one another.

"Did you wake anyone up—?" began Michael.

"Have you got over it, yet—?" said Sarah simultaneously.

And then they giggled, a bit.

"What I don't understand," said Michael, "is why I don't get nightmares. I don't sleep much, actually, but you'd think at least I'd dream."

"*I* do," said Sarah Jane. "I had an awful night, on Monday . . ."

"There *were* retributions," said Michael, "like he said, you know?"

And Sarah Jane glanced nervously over her shoulder. "Better not tell me the details," she said. "Let's go somewhere quieter."

She led him quickly around the side of the building, and soon they were skirting a sort of back porch, with a few dozing patients in wheelchairs. Michael could see the white physiotherapy unit a little way off.

"Sarah," he said.

"Yes?"

"D'you find it hard—with the War, I mean—at home?"

Sarah Jane smiled. "No," she said, "but I'm lucky, and I'll tell you why. With Dad so busy, and Mum in the hospital, I could be tap-dancing on the breakfast table every morning, for all anyone'd notice."

Michael laughed.

"Besides," said Sarah, "I don't really think they expect me to behave normally. I never have, before."

"What d'you mean?"

"Well," said Sarah Jane, "I just tell them things. I mean, anything that happens to me. I told Dad about the Sparrow, ages ago. But they don't take it seriously, you see. They never have. They think I'm playing. D'you know, before you, I'd never met anyone else who believed in magic?"

"Well, Simon does, you know. But it's a bit lonely, isn't it?"

"Not any more," said Sarah Jane, with a grin.

"Yes," said Michael. "Well."

"You know," said Sarah Jane, "I was *sure* you were in it, from the moment I saw you, and so I kept dropping hints. You dropped a few, yourself."

"Accidentally."

"But you *wouldn't* let your guard down!"

"Yes, well. To tell you the truth, at first I wasn't sure just whose side you were on, anyway."

"Well, that's flattering."

"I can't help being stupid," said Michael.

Reaching a sweet-smelling lawn, they glanced around them and sat down on it. Suddenly, it seemed that they had known each other forever. Michael said: "It's funny, I always get this feeling that none of it quite *clicks*, if you know what I mean. *Do* you?"

"Yes," said Sarah, "and I'll tell you how I see it. It's as though the whole thing is a jigsaw puzzle—with some missing pieces. And what drives you up the wall is that the missing pieces are the very ones that really tell you what the picture is. D'you know what we've got, Michael? About eighteen bits of sky and about twelve bits of ground. All the middle bit's gone."

Michael laughed, but it was a frustrated laugh.

"It's *SEI*, mainly," he said. "I always thought it was a word, from another language, didn't you?"

"*I* thought it was a code word," said Sarah Jane.

"Yes—well, you were closer than I was. It's initials, actually."

"*Initials?*" said Sarah Jane. "How'd you work that one out?"

"I didn't. Someone told me."

"Initials," said Sarah Jane thoughtfully.

Michael sighed. "I've been thinking," he said. "There's this Sympathy-Empathy business. I s'pose they've told you about that, have they?"

Sarah Jane laughed. "It has come up, from time to time," she said.

"Well, d'you think, you know—Sympathy, Empathy—there's the first two initials—"

"Michael!"

Her face had come alive.

"You think I'm right?" asked Michael tentatively.

"Well, yes, of course! And don't you see? If we helped first through Sympathy and then through Empathy, and if that's what the first two letters stand for—

119

well, that makes *SEI* a sort of formula. So the last letter must stand for—"

"Another way of helping," Michael supplied softly. They looked at each other, wondering whatever would happen next.

———

Sitting in a waiting room on the second floor, brooding and not reading magazines because he never did, Michael, for some reason, became extremely thirsty. It struck him that Sarah Jane was not likely to be back within half an hour, but just in case he told the nurse at the desk that he was going downstairs to the shop. Then, pawing through his blazer pockets for money, he popped downstairs.

But there was no shop on the first floor. Michael, checking the big directory near the elevators, thought the nurse *could* have told him. But then, she probably thought he meant all the way downstairs, for the shop, according to the directory, was on the ground. Michael clicked his tongue and took the next elevator down.

Having arrived at "G," however, he felt confused. It was all so very white. Blinking, Michael wandered up the hall, came across a split-level addition, and crossed into it. He found a maze of corridors, empty except for the occasional nurse, scurrying past in squeaky white shoes. Gosh, thought Michael, all these rooms, and all these patients! At some point, he stopped being thirsty and began simply to wander.

Eventually, he became aware that he was lost. But he was so dreamily alone, walking slowly down the white hallways, glancing into white doorways, that he felt unable to turn back. He had a vague feeling that he was supposed to be looking for something, seeking something out.

So it went on. Until, without knowing why, Michael glanced into one particular doorway and stopped.

In the room was a single bed. And, sitting up in it, was a man. He was dressed in a white surgical gown, and he had a white bandage around his eyes. Although sitting quite erect, he could almost have been asleep, for his features—long and refined—were set in an expression of remarkable calm. Drawn almost against his will, Michael crept over to the doorway. The man's face seemed to stir. Michael, suddenly frightened, turned to go. But then:

"Wait—please don't go. There *is* someone there, isn't there?"

"I—I'm sorry—" Michael faltered.

"Well, don't be afraid. Your name is—Michael—isn't it?" said the man, as if reading aloud. "Please come in."

Stunned, Michael obeyed him. "How . . . ?" he began.

"Well," said the man, "you are a Helper, aren't you?"

Michael felt the light break over him. "You're in it, too, then?"

"Yes, Michael. Could you help me, d'you think?"

Michael looked at him seriously. "What d'you have to do?" he said.

The man smiled blindly at him. "It's this operation," he said. "It may give me back my sight—or—it may not. It is . . . dangerous. That, Michael, is my mission. Sounds funny, doesn't it? You'd think it would only matter to me. But . . . apparently . . . it's important. A detail in the tapestry . . ." his smile became rather grim.

Michael's stomach lurched. "How—how d'you know?" he asked.

"Well," said the man, "I wasn't even in the War, until my accident. And then, while I was trying to decide whether or not to have this operation . . . something happened, I can't really tell you . . ."

"That's all right," Michael murmured.

" . . . and here I am. Just about to go in. I was expecting you, Michael."

"Were you?" said Michael huskily. And then, "My parents were in an accident."

"Yes, I know. Perhaps that's why we've met up. I need a bit of help, just now. I'm not at all sure what's going to happen to me, you see, and I'm . . ."

Michael, with a sort of gulp, turned quickly toward the window.

The man sighed and lay back on his pillows. "You needn't have moved, you know. You forget I can't see you." He paused, and said, "Thank you, Michael."

"What for?"

"Well, for your help, of course."

"H-help?" said Michael, turning suddenly back. "B-but I haven't done *anything*—"

"Oh, yes, you have," said the man. "You've hurt for me, haven't you? With that, Michael, I can manage."

"But—but—"

A nursing sister, very white and capable, bounded in through another door.

"Goodness, whoever let you in here? This man's just about to go into surgery. Out, thank you. No, you can't. Young man, I'd advise you—No, you *can't* . . ."

Michael, being gradually bustled out of the room, craned his neck to get a parting look. There was a younger nurse pumping something into the man's arm . . .

"Now, Mr. Havers, just relax . . ."

And Michael found the door shut in his face.

———

By the time Michael and Sarah Jane left the hospital, the world outside was a gently stirring dusk, light purple, fragrant, and cool. They decided to walk down to the main street, and get a taxi from there. It gave them more time.

But it was difficult to explain, even to Sarah Jane.

"I don't understand it myself," he said apologetically, when he had told her the story.

"Well," she said resignedly, "we never understand, do we?"

"No, I guess not. Perhaps we shouldn't even want to. I don't know. Only—well, *you* know." He stopped, looking at her. "What is it?"

Sarah Jane, with an odd expression on her face, walked on mechanically. The road, tree-lined and on a slope, was almost deserted. Michael began to feel a bit on edge.

"What *is* it?" he repeated.

"I'm sorry, Michael, I—it's just, I can hear footsteps. Behind."

Michael listened. "Only ours," he said reassuringly, after a moment.

Without noticing, however, they had begun to walk more quickly. Michael looked carefully over his shoulder.

"Anyway," he pressed, "there's nothing behind us."

But Sarah only walked on. "There's something following us," she said.

Something.

The dusk around them continued cool, fragrant, and noncommittal.

"Well, stop, then," said Michael suddenly, gripping her hand.

And they stopped.

But the footsteps didn't. And there was still nothing behind them.

They took off.

"We mustn't run," gasped Michael. "We'll only get tired, and we don't even know what we're running from."

"Who's running?" said Sarah Jane. "I'm just walking, *quickly.*"

Which they continued to do, all the way down the slope. But they didn't lose the footsteps. And now there was something else to worry about. Michael was sure he could feel a hand on his shoulder.

He was determined not to tell her. It could only be his imagination, after all, and he didn't want to make her any worse. But the hand, light, tingling, and invisible, lingered. And Michael, walking *very* quickly down the road, was beginning to think he couldn't hold out any longer when Sarah, in a great gulp, caught her breath . . .

"Wh-what's wrong?" he demanded.

She stopped quite suddenly and looked up at him. "Michael," she said, "someone just pulled my hair."

Michael, with an odd, scraping gesture at his shoulder, said unsteadily: "Something's trying to frighten us."

Sarah Jane looked nervously at him. "What's wrong with your shoulder?" she asked.

"I'd rather not say. Look, Sarah, we must keep calm . . ."

"No," said a tight little voice in his ear, "don't do that. *Panic.*"

Michael's heart leapt to his throat.

"Wh-what's wrong?"

"N-nothing. C-come on, we've got to think of some-thing—"

"No, don't *think*," said the tight little voice. "*Panic.*"

"Look," said Michael, "you shut up!"

"*Michael!*"

"Oh, not *you*—"

But Sarah Jane was off down the road, dragging him behind her. "Come on!" she said, through gritted teeth.

"Wh-where are we—?"

"The church—we've got to—"

"The *church?*" cried Michael.

"Oh, no, don't go *there*," said the tight little voice. "Horrible place, that. Just *panic*—"

"Look, bugger off, will you?"

But luckily Sarah Jane didn't hear him. They raced down the slope, running properly, now, wanting only to escape. There was nothing but bumping discomfort, and fear, and the church at the base of the slope which, for some horrible moments, seemed to get farther and farther away.

But then there was Albert Street. And after that, the park; and the rectory; and finally, the church.

They stumbled up stone steps, clambered into the cloistered quiet. Michael thought he heard a squeal, then silence. The hand was gone.

They threw themselves against the bookstall, puffing hard. And the Sparrow, emerging vaguely from the interior, said: "I'll get him for you."

He slipped out of the church and disappeared.

The Hill

Thursday afternoon was cricket. Michael, thinking intently about identity, was not what you would call a competent fielder. It was a relief to get home and drink water in the kitchen.

"Michael, honestly," said his grandmother, scurrying in to save a stewy mess on the verge of boiling over. "You could've turned it down." And then, looking up at him, "Those whites are *floating* on you."

Michael smiled at her absently.

"How was cricket, anyway?"

"Not much good."

"Oh?"

"Well," said Michael cryptically, "I wasn't—sort of—*noticing* the ball . . ."

"Oh, I see," said Mrs. Devine quietly. "Anyway, dinner's nearly ready. Could you pop up and tell Jilly?"

Michael rinsed his glass and "popped" obediently upstairs. He poked his head through the door and got as far as: "Gran says dinner's nearly . . ." before he registered Sarah Jane Yardley sitting next to Jilly at the desk. For a moment, Juliet went to the wind.

"I thought you weren't coming," he said.

Sarah Jane, sitting there with her bottle green pinafore

and her long dark braid, made faces at him. But Jilly, who was marking the younger girl's exercises, didn't appear to notice.

"Hi, Mike," she said, grimacing as she crossed something out. "Dinner ready, did you say?"

Michael, looking at Sarah Jane, said: "More or less."

"Well, it's six o'clock," said Jilly, glancing at her watch. "That'll do us, I think, Sarah Jane. You staying for dinner?"

"Yes, please. Dad's at the hospital. He won't be here till half past. And Mrs. Devine said . . ."

"That's okay," said Jilly. "No bother." And she got up, smoothing down the green tartan skirt. "I'd better just see if Gran needs any help."

Michael waited for Jilly to go. Then said: "Has anything happened?"

"No," said Sarah Jane, "but I've been thinking . . ."

"So've I," said Michael grimly. "What've you been thinking about?"

"The church, mainly."

"The church?" said Michael.

"Yes. I headed for it instinctively yesterday. I just knew we'd be safe there. And we were."

"So?"

Sarah Jane looked steadily at him. "You ought to read a few fairy tales," she said.

"We already have an expert in residence," said Michael. "Why?"

"Because this is an *old* one," said Sarah Jane. "Evil can never follow you into consecrated ground."

Evil, thought Michael.

"Oh," he said aloud. Then: "Come on, they'll start getting ideas."

They scuttled downstairs.

Robyn, hooking a loaded coat hanger on the door, glanced up at them and wheezed.

"Oh, Robyn," said Mrs. Devine, "you're not getting tight, are you? I do hate you using that Ventilin."

Michael, eyeing the dress as it hung, beautiful under its plastic cover, on the door, said: "What's up with you, Sunshine?"

Robyn, fingering her script, looked up. "Don't you know anything?" she said.

This was plainly rhetorical.

"Your dress rehearsal, hey?"

"Yes, of course. And you should've *known*, Mikey."

"A momentary lapse, my dear. A thousand apologies."

"It's at the Railway Institute," Robyn pursued, more or less appeased. "You really ought to come."

"Who, me? What for?"

"Well, to watch, of course. Miss Thom won't mind. She said she *wanted* an audience. And my friends all like you."

Well, that was true. A bit too true for comfort. Little girls, thought Michael, gently derisive.

"But I've got work to do," he began, on his last legs. "I can't just—"

"I'd love to see it," said Sarah Jane. "Would you mind if I came, too?"

"*Too?*" said Michael. "Look, I haven't said—"

"Oh, *do*," said Robyn, delighted.

"But what about your father?" said Michael.

"I can call him at the hospital. Then he can come and pick us all up."

"That's not necessary, dear," said Mrs. Devine, from the kitchen. "Tell your father not to worry. Robyn needs the audience. I'll drive you home afterward."

So that was settled, and Michael was stuck.

———

It was late-night shopping; the street was busy. Like one of Jilly's patchwork quilts, thought Michael—with a square for the chocolate-smeared toddler, another for the father minding the pram outside the supermarket, a bright one for the lights and bells of the pinball parlour, and yet another for the gentle, hops-scented hum of the pub.

Michael and Robyn and Sarah Jane waded through the mob. Until, about halfway down, Michael heard a sound, soaring tremulously over the hubbub. It was a small, singing voice.

As it turned out, the voice was standing on the corner. A boy, small and dark and thin, with a large biscuit tin at his feet, was busking outside the fish shop. I'M SAVING UP FOR MY TRIP TO CHINA said the felt-penned sign on the tin, and he already had a coin or two, to put it mildly. He sang, in his thin, sweet voice, some old folksong that Michael only half-remembered.

Michael stopped, confused. The boy was dark and slight, so was he: there was something in that. And the boy, catching his interested eye, gave him a sort of look . . .

"He's only a busker," said Sarah Jane, who knew the workings of his mind.

"Yes," but . . ." Michael searched his pockets. "Rats, I haven't got anything to give him."

"He'll manage," said Sarah Jane dryly. "Come on, Michael. Your sister's way ahead—"

"But he's one of *us*," Michael hissed. "I'm sure he is."

Sarah Jane eyed him speculatively. "Even so," she said, firmly, "there's nothing much we can do about it."

But Michael had found a coin. Sarah Jane tagged after him.

"Wait *on*," she said.

Michael dropped the coin and looked up furtively. The boy smiled at him, in a way that seemed curiously understanding.

"Thank you" was all he said. But it was enough.

Michael, running with Sarah Jane across the street, said happily: "He *was*, you know."

Sarah Jane looked at him.

"Trouble with you is," she said, "you don't know what *is* the War and what's not."

Michael, thinking of something the Sparrow had said, murmured: "Is anything *not* the War?"

———

The Railway Institute was friendly in the dying sunlight, its side door standing open. Michael, Robyn, and Sarah Jane, their footsteps echoing across the floorboards, looked around them. Robyn sneezed.

"It's the dust," she explained. "Look," pointing into the corner, "resin."

"Come on, Robyn," said Michael. "And couldn't you put this—dress—backstage or something? It's heavy."

Miss Thom, dark, with a glossy bun and great, sagging eyes, came out from behind the curtain. "Hurry up, Robyn, dear, you're late. We're having a go at some make-up." She nodded cheerfully at Michael and Sarah Jane. "Come to watch, have you? Jolly good. Come on, Princess."

Robyn, with her costume slung over her shoulder,

scuttled like a curly mouse across the floorboards. Miss Thom hustled her off behind the curtains. Michael looked on after them.

"It's pretty big, this place," he remarked.

"It makes me want to dance," said Sarah Jane. And she kicked out in a sudden arabesque. "I used to do ballet," she added, fidgeting around the floor.

Michael, following her with his eyes, said: "I told you about the dress, didn't I?"

"It's strange, really, isn't it? Not because of the lady— we're used to that sort of thing. But more because of Robyn. And the play. Gee," she added, with a turn and a stumble, "d'you think, p'raps—because of the dress— something funny might happen?"

"With the play, you mean? I hope not. Robyn's got enough to worry about, with that wicked father of hers."

Sarah Jane, who had glanced through the script on her way down, giggled. Then she did a series of pirouettes across the floor.

"That's clever," said Michael.

"Yes, I . . ." and she paused, a bit puffed. Then, quite suddenly, her expression changed. "Hello!" she said.

Michael spun around. But it was only a dog, panting in the doorway, long-haired and noble-looking.

"Oh, the lovely thing!" said Sarah Jane. Apparently sensing approval, the dog padded over to her. "Oh, Michael, isn't he beautiful?"

He was, rather, panting away as Sarah patted him. Michael, melting, came over and felt in the long hair of his friendly neck for a collar. But there was none.

"He couldn't be a stray," said Michael. "He's too well looked after. I wonder whoever let him out without a collar on?"

"He's very friendly," said Sarah Jane, "aren't you, mate? He can stay in here, can't he?"

"Why not?" said Michael. "He might find his own way home, anyway.

But the dog, at least at first, showed no signs of departure. They decided it was unfair to encourage him, and so went off hunting for some chairs to sit on. But when they came back, the dog was still there, as if waiting for them. They placed their chairs by the door, so that they could enjoy the evening air, and he settled calmly at their feet.

"You adopted us, fella?" said Michael to the dog, rubbing his fur. "Oh, well. I hope you're not bored."

And Miss Thom, looking worried, bustled out from behind the curtains. "We're starting now," she said, looking distractedly around her for a chair.

Michael stood, hurriedly. "Look, you have this one," he said. "I'll just . . ."

"Oh, thank you—Michael, is it? I'd better take this down the back—see if I can hear them properly."

Michael leaned against the door frame and stroked the dog with his foot. The curtain opened jerkily, and a boy of about Robyn's age, in school uniform, stepped out toward the middle of the stage.

"*Far, far away* . . ." he began in a singsong.

"Wait," said Miss Thom, springing from her chair. "Where's your costume, Brian?"

"At the dry cleaner's," said Brian.

"I don't know why I didn't notice you before," said Miss Thom with a sigh. "Never mind, can't be helped. But you must stand on the *side*, Brian, or we won't be able to see Robyn, when she comes out. Could we have that again, please?"

The curtain began to twitch, and Miss Thom said hurriedly, "No, no, don't shut them on him. Go back, please, Brian, and pretend they've just opened."

Brian moved carefully to the left side of the stage, stood on one leg, and recommenced: *"Far, far away, in a land beyond the morning star . . ."*

And Robyn, in the dress, was suddenly the Princess again.

"She's awfully good," whispered Sarah Jane after a moment. But Michael, deep in thought, only nodded. For it was odd—the dress, and what she had said the other day when she was in it. *Identity,* thought Michael. *Melting.* He wondered, suddenly, if the dress was trying to tell him something. He suggested this, rather tentatively, to Sarah Jane.

"Identity?" she whispered confusedly. "I don't understand, Michael."

Neither did he.

The play stumbled on.

"I am the Fairy Godmother," announced a pretty little thing in a pink tutu, as Michael looked thoughtfully out into the darkening evening. The dog got up suddenly and stood in the doorway. For a moment they thought he'd had enough. But he wasn't going, not yet. He turned around twice, sniffed at the evening air, and sat back down at Sarah's feet.

And Miss Thom said: "That's lovely, dear, but you must speak *up*—"

"But I'm supposed to be sighing—" the Fairy Godmother protested.

"Yes, but you must sigh *audibly,* dear, or no one'll know how good you are! That bit again, please."

A cool breeze wafted about them. Michael shivered

and pulled on his sweater. The play continued at a walk.

"*I can't tell you that,*" roared the Prince, freckled and brown-eyed. "*I promised.*"

"So *what!*" cackled the Wicked Witch, rather well. "*You humans and your stupid promises!*"

"*Promises,*" said the Prince loftily, "*are sacred . . .*"

The dog, restless, got up and walked out a little way into the darkness. He trotted back to Michael and looked up at him rather intently. Michael stroked his head.

"What's up, fella?" he whispered.

But the dog only trotted back into the night. Michael, shivering, followed him. And Sarah Jane came curiously to the doorway.

Outside, it was starry. Michael, wading through the not-very-well-trimmed grass, was just beginning to wonder what he thought he was doing, when he caught sight of the hill.

It wasn't new to him or anything; he had often seen it before. Long and low and grassy, it overlooked the railway line and was rather pretty, as hills go. But tonight it was different. There were lights, golden and soft pink, glinting at him. Was it—a fair of some sort? Michael wondered. The dog ran rings around him. Michael went back to the hall.

Sarah Jane was sitting down again, staring at the stage. Michael popped his head around the door.

"Come for a walk?" he whispered. And held out his hand.

Sarah Jane widened her sea-gray eyes. She glanced at the back of the hall, took his hand, and followed him out into the night.

"What is it?"

"I don't know. I think it's some sort of fair. P'raps the

134

dog belongs there. He certainly wants us to come."

"A fair?" said Sarah Jane. "Where?"

"On the hill. I'm just guessing. You'll see for yourself in a minute."

They walked on, a little breathless, through the damp, breezy night.

"Oh," said Sarah Jane presently, "lights!"

And Michael said: "That's funny. It's a full moon."

They began to hurry, even to stumble a little in the dark. A grassy slope rose gradually from beneath them. At first, they didn't notice the dark shapes on the hillside. Then, suddenly, Michael tripped on something and heard a yelp.

"Sorry!" he said.

"That's all right," said the dog.

Michael gave a sort of squeak. "It—it *talked*!"

"Michael, shut *up*!" said Sarah Jane, preoccupied. "Look!"

For the hillside, bathed in a soft, many-colored light, was a-twitch with dogs and cats. They were lying, sitting, standing all around, apparently too busy to fight. And all of them were gazing in silence at the hilltop.

Michael gasped. Up in front of them were people, wonderful people—dancing, smiling—but as plainly inhuman as the moon was white. They were tall and slender and tremulous, blanched as if moon-burned. Their clothes, soft pink and gold and pastel green, and their veils, like cobwebs, and their wisps of long, silvery hair, drifted, rhythmic, in the breeze. And there were flowers, everywhere, flowers and the scent of flowers. It was as if the moonlight had come alive.

Then, the moonlight seemed to speak. A whisper, all around them.

"You see, it is not all pain, to help," it sighed. "And all of us have our missions." Then the dancing people faded, dissolved into the starry night.

For a moment, it seemed very dark. Then, as his eyes got used to the light, Michael saw cats and dogs trotting off peaceably to begin, or to end, the business of the night. *Their* dog was nowhere to be seen.

———

Later, after a quick trip out to Coleridge Heights, the Devines spilled into the darkened flat.

"Toast and tea!" said Robyn, through a quick, wide-eyed yawn. Her face, all odd and painted-looking, shone under the electric light.

"You ought to be in bed," said Mrs. Devine.

But Michael, yawning himself, said kindly: "Fair go! She hasn't finished the interrogation yet."

"We have ways of making you talk," said Robyn. "You did see the last bit, didn't you?"

"I was there for the last ten minutes or so," said Mrs. Devine, filling the kettle, "and I thought you were marvelous, Robyn."

"So did Miss Thom," said Jilly. "She came over to us. Was the end the best bit or the worst?"

"Somewhere in between," said Robyn. "I like the middle best, but the end's okay. Except the end hasn't got as much me in it."

Michael slid off the table and went into the living room. Tripping over the cat, he wondered, as he fumbled at the light switch, if Hamlet had been with the group on the hill. He looked narrowly at him, but Hamlet only blinked sleepily. If he *had* been there, he wasn't saying, anyway.

"The Wicked Witch was rather good," Jilly was saying in the kitchen. "But I don't like the Narrator, much, Robyn. Is he really going to wear his school uniform?"

Michael laughed softly. Then his eyes fell on the bird cage.

"Oh, I don't know," said Mrs. Devine's voice. "At least his diction was good. You could hear every word that child said."

"But it sounded so *boring*, in a monotone, like that."

"Not a monotone. More a singsong, really . . ."

Michael went slowly to the cage. The budgie, lying on the bottom with a dull reflection of the light in its still, black eye, was as dead as only a caged bird can be. There was a note, tied with a red ribbon, round its neck:

WE HAVE STARTED ON YOUR HOUSE.

Michael, fumbling with frantic haste at the little wire door, thrust his hand in and tore the ribbon off.

"D'you want some toast, Michael?"

He shut the door; he scrunched the note in his fist. He said huskily, "No, thanks. Jilly, listen—"

"But the costume looked lovely, didn't it? Talk about *luck*."

"That's for sure," said Mrs. Devine. "But Robyn's always been like that."

"Like what?" said Robyn, suspicious.

And Michael, pale, came into the doorway. "Gran— I—er—"

"Oh, there you are. Have some milk, at least, it should help you sleep."

Michael shook his head, swallowed.

"What's up?" said Jilly.

"The bird's dead," he said.

Chaos

riday was singularly uneventful. But Saturday was a different matter.

Michael was awakened by a knock on his bedroom door. It was an odd way to wake; people tended to barge in, especially if they thought you were asleep. Michael stumbled over to the door.

"Who . . . ?" he began.

It was Simon. "Listen, mate, you've got a visitor."

"A *visitor*? What's the time?"

" 'Bout half-past six. Come on, he's waiting . . ."

Mystified, Michael pulled on his bathrobe and followed him up the stairs, through the laundry, out into the hall. Simon stood back, near the stairs, almost shy. Michael threw him a questioning glance, gestured toward the front door, and, receiving Simon's nod, shrugged his shoulders and opened it.

The visitor was in the front garden. On a white horse. He had a cloak of purple velvet and a golden sword at his hip. He wore a light gray padded tunic, with gray stockings, and a round velvet cap topped his glossy brown hair.

"Good sir," he said, in ringing tones. "Knowest thou a fair maiden by the name of Rapunzel?"

Michael blinked. "Hmm?"

"Rapunzel. I believe she's locked up in some tower around here. It's an unusual name, I know, but—"

"Did you say *Rapunzel?*"

"You know her, then?"

"Know her?" Michael rubbed his eyes and glanced nervously back at the house. "Look, I'm sorry, but I think you're in the wrong fairy tale," he said.

The Prince looked vaguely about him. "Oh, *dear.* Dreadfully sorry; I've got you up for nothing. Steady, Beauty!" he added softly, as the white horse fidgeted beneath him. "What's this one like, anyway?"

Michael sighed. "Just beginning to get nasty, I think."

The Prince looked sympathetic. "Bad luck, old chap! Anything I could do?"

Michael smiled at him. "Thanks, but—"

"Well, I *have* got my hands full, with Rapunzel, I suppose. Never mind. These things always have a happy ending, you know."

"Yes," said Michael. "Yes, I suppose they do."

The Prince gathered up his reins. "Must be off," he said. "Good luck, then!"

"Yes. Yes, same to you . . ."

And the Prince rode off into nowhere.

Simon, still standing near the stairs, gazed disbelievingly at him as he shut the door, and said, "Did—did I see . . ."

Michael smiled tiredly at him. "Believe me, you saw it," he said.

———

In the kitchen, Michael stared drowsily out the window, sipping tea. It was now about eight o'clock, and the flat was still silent and sleepy. Except for Robyn, poking her head around the doorway.

"Michael?"

Her voice, which seemed to lisp even when she wasn't trying to say an "s," was excited and confidential. Michael looked up, surprised.

"Well, come on!" she said impatiently.

She pulled him by the sleeve into her pink and white bedroom—lavender-hankies-muddle-and-mess. The pink-curtained window was open.

"What is it?"

"*Look*, Moriarty! On the ledge, silly. No, over there—see it?"

Michael leaned out the window. "It's a sparrow," he muttered, staring at the little concrete ledge.

"Smarter than the average bear!" said Robyn. "Now, rescue it, Mikey."

"Who, me?"

"Oh, go on. If we leave it out there, the cat'll get it."

"Hamlet? He's too smart to go risking his neck. Anyway, it's dead, isn't it?"

"No, no," said Robyn, being witty. "'E's restin'."

"Look, could you be sensible for two seconds?"

But at that point the sparrow moved.

"*See?*"

Michael sighed, pushed resignedly at the window. "Oh, all right." He straddled the sill and slid down onto the ledge.

It was odd, really. Because when the sparrow saw him, it seemed to recover a little, instead of panicking. Its head turned toward him with a weak little flick, and it fixed him with a bright black eye. Michael gathered it up in his palm, felt a tiny, terrified heartbeat in its

140

feathery breast, and handed it carefully to Robyn through the open window. Then he glanced up to catch sight of Jilly leaning out of the window above, her face paper-white.

"Michael, whatever are you doing? Come back in this *minute!*"

Michael shrugged and obeyed her. Talk about panic stations, he thought. By the time he had pulled himself back in, she was clattering down the stairs.

"Michael, *honestly!* You almost gave me a heart attack!"

"Oh, my gosh!" cried Michael. "Is there a doctor in the house?"

Robyn, nursing the sparrow in her cupped hands, said: "Shh! You'll frighten it!"

Jilly forgot to be angry. "What've you got there, Rob?"

"It's a sparrow," said Michael, peering down at it. "It was on the ledge. Looks sick, doesn't it?"

"Oh, dear, yes."

"Couldn't we feed it?" said Robyn. "We can put it in the budgie's cage . . ."

"No, don't do that," said Michael quickly.

"It *would* be a bit crass," Jilly agreed, misunderstanding his reluctance. "Never mind, I'll get a shoe box."

They found one in the bottom of Robyn's wardrobe, with the tissue paper from her last pair of new shoes still in it. Jilly lined the box with newspaper and padded one end with cotton from the bathroom. Michael filled an eggcup with water and put it in a corner. It looked a cozy little convalescent home. But the sparrow, gray and striped like something out of an army, just wasn't interested. It huddled on the newspaper, dejected and motionless.

"Might he eat birdseed, d'you think?" asked Jilly.

"Try bread crumbs," Michael suggested. "That's what they eat in the park."

Then Robyn, peering into the box, said suddenly: "D'you know, I think he's hurt his little wing! He's got it hanging sort of limp, like an arm, almost . . ."

Michael choked. Robyn, deciding to throw around a little elementary first aid, gave him a hefty thwack between the shoulder blades. This didn't exactly improve things. Jilly, alarmed, said: "Not so *rough!*"

And Michael gasped: "I'm—all—right. Just don't—do that again . . ."

He turned away, to cough in peace—and to think, quickly.

For it might *not* be him. There were plenty of sparrows around; it was not unlikely that one should get hurt and turn up on Robyn's window ledge. But then, he couldn't be sure. And besides, the bird was sick. If it *were* an enchantment, and the bird should—snuff it—would that mean that the Sparrow . . . ?

Michael fretted. "We'll have to get him to the vet," he said abruptly.

"The vet?" said Jilly. "Michael, that's expensive."

However, it was the only way of touching wood, until he was sure. Perhaps—perhaps if the bird got well, the Sparrow would come back.

Mrs. Devine, standing in the doorway in her blue flannel bathrobe, gazed in at them with her blank morning face. "What's going on here?"

"Oh, Gran," said Jilly. "It's this bird . . ."

"The budgie, you mean? But didn't Michael take him—"

"Not the *budgie*," said Robyn. "This is a sparrow. A sick one. We found him, Gran . . ."

Michael, chewing on a fingernail, made a quick decision. He went downstairs.

———

"Are you sure you don't mind?" asked Michael, standing by Simon's phone, with the receiver clasped to his chest.

"Of course not," said Simon abstractedly, sketching rapidly. "Go ahead."

Michael, who could still remember the number, dialed quickly. But this time it wasn't Sarah who answered.

"Hello, this is Peter Fanshawe speaking. Is Sarah Jane there, please?"

Simon dropped his charcoal and looked up quizzically.

"Sarah? Listen, you've got to get over here. Something's happened. Well, I don't think I'd better say. Yes. All right. Thanks. Bye."

He placed the receiver back on the hook and stood for a moment, thinking.

"Well, hello, Pete. Pleased to meet you," said Simon, with a glint in his eye, and went on sketching.

"It's not funny," said Michael gravely. "But thanks a lot for the phone."

Simon just smiled to himself and stood back for a moment, surveying his work. He was sketching the Prince. From memory.

———

Upstairs, they were eating a distracted sort of breakfast.

"Where is he?" Michael demanded, still buttoning his shirt.

"On the sideboard," said Mrs. Devine. "Please sit down, Michael."

Michael obeyed her, unhappily. He wished he could

get the sparrow alone for a moment. "I *can* take him up to the vet, can't I?"

Mrs. Devine sighed. "You kids. Heavens, when I was a child, we certainly didn't have the money to go chasing up doctors for animals. We were lucky if we got a doctor for *ourselves*."

"The Good Old Days," said Michael.

"Honestly, Michael, a wild bird . . ."

"Well, I said I'd pay for it."

"And there goes your savings down the drain."

"It's *my* money, Gran!"

Robyn drained her milk glass. "I have to go," she said. "They're starting at nine."

"At nine?" said Jilly. "You should've left half an hour ago."

"Yes," said Robyn, "but I didn't know we were going to find a sick sparrow, did I? I wish I could go to the vet with Michael."

"Now, don't *you* start," said Mrs. Devine. "If Michael must go, I think he can manage on his own."

At that point the phone rang, and Mrs. Devine went to answer it.

"I'm so jittery," said Jilly with a little laugh. "I think I'll have to make a cake."

This was what she always did when she was nervous. She said it made her feel better. Michael shrugged. "Whatever turns you on, Sunshine," he said.

They listened, for a moment, to their grandmother's voice being annoyed, then surprised, then worried. Jilly, getting out flour and eggs, said to Michael, "I'll put in, if you like, for the vet. It shouldn't be too much."

"Gee, thanks," said Michael. He suddenly decided to ask Simon if he'd drive them.

His grandmother reappeared in the doorway. "That was Uncle Max," she said worriedly. "I'm afraid your great-aunt Alice has taken a turn."

"A *turn*?" said Robyn.

"It's her heart," said Mrs. Devine. "They admitted her early this morning. Jilly, I'll really have to go and see what I can do . . ."

Kind Juliet went over to her. "Of course you will, Gran. We'll be all right."

"You'll have to look after the flats for me. Oh dear! I wonder when the next train leaves? Are you sure you'll be all right, Jilly?"

"Perfectly," said Jilly firmly. "I'm eighteen, for heaven's sake. Don't you worry about a thing."

But Robyn's lip was wobbling. "Does that mean you won't be here for the play?" she asked shakily.

"Now, you settle down, there's a good girl. I'll just have to see how poor Alice is. She's my sister after all, you know, Robyn. Heavens, where's that timetable?" she added, drifting with Jilly into the next room. "I'll need to pack an overnight bag, at least."

Still halfway into tears, Robyn tagged after them. "What'll I do, Gran?"

Michael, biting his lip, glanced over at the sparrow. "Why won't you speak to me?" he hissed.

But the sparrow, eyeing him in a shiny black sort of way, was silent.

———

"To the vet?" said Simon mixing paints. "Oh, all right, then. What's the rush?"

"It's Gran," Michael explained hurriedly. "She'll want you to drive her to the station in about half an hour."

"Busy, this morning, aren't I? But you're supposed to be meeting little what's-her-name, aren't you?"

Michael, glancing out the window, saw long dark hair and jeans get out of her father's car.

"Speak of the devil," he said in relief. "Here she is."

He seized the sparrow's box and careered out into the hall. Simon, with a sigh, wiped his hands with turpentine on a rag and went upstairs to get the keys.

"Good morning, Michael," said Mrs. Beasley, with a shopping-basket over her arm. "Where're you off to?"

"Hmm?" said Michael. "Oh, the vet's."

"Your little budgie sick, is he?" said Mrs. Beasley, glancing at the shoe box.

"Oh, no," said Michael, halfway out the door. "He's dead."

Mrs. Beasley looked blankly after him. And Simon, coming briskly down the stairs, caught her eye.

"Don't ask me," he murmured, "I'm only the driver!" and hurried out to the car.

"Your gran wasn't too pleased," he said, as they pulled out of the drive with Sarah Jane sitting next to him and Michael nursing the shoe box in the back. "It isn't exactly tactful, Mike. It looks as if you're more interested in a bird than in your dear old Auntie Alice."

Michael briefly contemplated the sort of "words" he might expect when he got home. Except, Gran would probably be gone by then, anyway. And by the time she got back . . .

"I can't help it," he said regretfully.

Simon flicked on the blinker. His hands, resting on the wheel, were still flecked with blue paint. "What's the fuss, anyway?" he said.

Michael coughed. "We—er—think he's a friend." He patted the box.

Simon glanced in the rearview mirror and raised an eyebrow. "Fair enough," he sighed. "Your funeral."

"It won't come to that, we hope," said Sarah Jane. "Did anything happen yesterday, Michael?"

"Not a thing," said Michael despondently.

"Dad wasn't exactly crazy about me coming up," said Sarah Jane. "I had to tell him I had this pressing problem with my French assignment. And then he said, Wasn't I bothering Juliet too much, and I'd be wearing out my welcome, and all that. And he asked me who Peter Fanshawe was, of course."

"*Oh*," said Michael.

"Yes. You know, it really would be much simpler if you used your own name."

Michael shrugged. "I was going to be Mary Fanshawe's brother," he said. "What'd you tell him?"

"Well, that you were a friend. Only now, of course, he thinks—well, you know what he thinks."

Michael grimaced. Simon, silent, turned the car into Elizabeth Street.

The vet's surgery—a small, brick building attached to a group of shops—did not appear to be very busy.

"Anywhere here'll do," said Michael. "We can walk."

"No, that's all right," said Simon, preoccupied. He did a neat U-turn and dropped them off at the door. "I can't wait," he said. "Can you get home from here?"

"We'll be all right," said Michael, cradling the shoe box, while Sarah Jane shut the door. "Thanks a lot, Simon."

Simon, with one eye on the rearview mirror, nodded

a little worriedly at them and drove off.

"Okay," said Michael. "Come on."

They went in.

The waiting room smelled faintly of flea powder. It housed a Persian cat, a baby dachshund, and an unidentifiable something in a wooden crate. Michael and Sarah Jane glanced about them and sat down. The dachshund lady smiled, the child with the crate sucked his thumb, and a dog in the next room yelped, piteously. It was a bit depressing.

Then the door opened. An elderly lady, her arms full of a large, hairy dog, scuttled into the waiting room.

"He's all right, really," she explained apologetically. "He's only been having injections."

"Next, please," said a voice from within the surgery. The Persian, with its bearded, academic-looking master, made its stately way in. Michael, who hated waiting, lifted the lid of the box and peered in at the sparrow, which was continuing in a stable condition. He wondered whatever would happen next.

"Does he look any better?" said Sarah Jane.

Michael, depressed, shook his head. He said, softly, "I was wondering, if we got him better, whether he mightn't be able to turn himself back."

"That's if it *is* him," said Sarah Jane.

The Persian came out, and the dachshund went in.

Michael, brushing his hands on his jeans, handed the box to Sarah Jane and wandered over to look at the newspaper clippings on the notice board: RSPCA SHORT OF FUNDS. A GLOSSARY OF VETERINARY TERMS. CHOOSING A PET. SEALS A DYING RACE. KEEPING YOUR PET HEALTHY. Michael had not been at the vet's since Hamlet's operation, three years ago.

Like everything else he hadn't seen for three years, it looked smaller than he remembered. He chewed a nail, stared into space. The dachshund came out, and the crate went in.

Michael came back and sat down. He stared at the fluffed-up huddle of feathers in the box and sighed dismally.

"Well," said Sarah Jane, "it might not be him."

"But what if it is?"

The vet, in the doorway, said: "May I help you?"

They hurried in.

"When did you find him?" the vet asked.

"This morning," said Michael. "About eight o'clock."

"Hmm," said the vet. "He's not very nervous. It's as if he knows you . . ."

Michael coughed. The vet scooped into the box, held the bird in his cupped hands. "He's injured his wing," he observed, "but it's not broken, I don't think. It's an unusual injury. Birds of this type don't normally behave this way."

He put the sparrow gently back in the box and went to fetch a glass eyedropper from a cabinet in the corner.

"Have you given him anything to eat?"

"We tried," said Michael, "but he wouldn't."

"I see. Well, this'll give him a little strength, and it ought to ease the pain, also."

He unscrewed the bottle, filled the dropper, and took the bird into his hand. Then he gave it a couple of drops, which the sparrow swallowed in throbbing gulps.

"Right!" said the vet. "Just watch him, for a moment, will you? I've left something in my car, I'm afraid."

He left them in the chilly white surgery. Michael and Sarah Jane looked at one another and then at the sparrow.

"What do we do, now?" said Michael bleakly.

"Just wait, I suppose," said Sarah Jane. And added, "What a funny smell!"

The shoe box, poised on the table, had begun to spew a fine, acrid stream of black smoke. And then, suddenly, a dark figure sat before them on the table.

As if there had been some type of explosion, he threw an arm up to shield his face and cried out a single, foreign word. Then, peering over his wrist, he saw them, and recovered abruptly.

"Devine!" he said. "Yardley! I am sorry; I thought . . ."

"Quick," said Sarah Jane, the first to recover, "we've got to hide you."

"Hide?" said the Sparrow, through what appeared to be a splitting headache. "Oh, yes . . ."

"Take him out," said Michael. "The vet'll be back in a minute."

As, indeed, he was.

"Oh," he said, staring at the squashed shoe box.

"He got better," said Michael. "He flew away."

"Oh," said the vet again. "Where's your little friend?"

Michael bit his lip. "She—er—got upset. She was quite attached to him."

"Oh, I see," said the vet. "I'm sorry." And paused. "Excuse me," he said, after a moment, "but you shouldn't smoke in my surgery, you know."

Michael gave an apologetic swipe at a faint tail of smoke. "Sorry," he said. "Will I pay now?"

But the vet, eyeing him oddly through his kind, Chinese eyes, just shook his head. "That's all right," he said. "I never charge for wild things. Thanks for bringing him in."

"Gee whiz," said Michael, retreating hurriedly. "Thanks a lot . . ."

"Where is he?" Michael panted.

"Gone," said Sarah huskily. "He said he couldn't afford to stay any longer. He thanked us—he said to tell you—for—for everything—"

"For *everything*?" Michael echoed, in dismay. He stared out tensely at the passing cars, banging one fist against his side. "Don't cry," he said, after a moment.

"S-sorry. He just looked so—so—"

"Listen, there's nothing we can do now. Next thing, your Dad'll be on the phone, and then *I'll* get it. Can I put you on a bus?"

"Y-yes—"

"Well, then, you go home, and I'll call if anything happens."

"Promise?"

"Yes, of course. You can come to church tomorrow, can't you?"

"I think so."

"Well, look. Come up to my place at about nine, and we can walk down, all right?"

He waved her off on the Coleridge Heights Special.

———

Juliet was in the kitchen, only just completing the promised cake. She was, unfortunately, in the grip of one of her rare bad moods. Michael stood gingerly in the doorway.

"And where've you been?"

"The vet's. I told you I was going."

The cake clattered into the oven.

Jilly said: "Honestly, Michael. That was before Auntie Alice—"

"Well, I don't see what I could've done about *that*—"

"You could've been here, that's all. People expect you to be around, you know, during family crises."

"The done thing, I suppose," said Michael.

Jilly just looked at him. "What happened, anyway?" she said after a moment.

"It got better," said Michael. "We let it go."

"A miracle recovery," said Jilly. "I see. Anyway, Gran's gone. Simon drove us up to the station. Just caught the ten forty-two. She's going to call when she gets there. Hand me that sugar, will you?"

Jilly, slamming cupboard doors, began to clean up. Michael looked guilty.

"D'you want me to—"

"And I haven't the slightest idea what to get for lunch. Canned spaghetti, I suppose. The world's greatest cook!" Jilly, wiping down the stove, burned herself on the hot-plate. "Oh!"

Then someone clattered up the stairs, banged into the flat. Robyn filled the kitchen and, looking around at them, began suddenly to howl. Jilly threw down the tea towel and went over to her.

"Robyn, what's wrong? What's the matter?"

"My—my play—"

"Your play?"

"It's—it's Ricky Simpson. He's *sick*!"

"Sick?" Jilly echoed, in consternation. "But he's the Prince, isn't he?"

Speechless, Robyn nodded.

"What's wrong with him?" said Michael.

"Br-bronchitis . . ."

"But it's on Tuesday night, isn't it?" said Jilly.

Robyn snuffled. Michael fished out a hankie and Jilly mopped her up.

"Oh!" she wailed. "He *can't* be better by then."

"Oh, I don't know," said Jilly. "What'd Miss Thom say?"

"She—she's going to call it off."

"Call it off?" said Jilly.

"Look," said Michael, "just dry up for a moment, will you? Even if she does call it off, she'll still do it eventually, won't she? And then at least Gran'd be here to see you."

"Yes," said Jilly. "Not so bad."

But Robyn shook her head. "We b-booked the hall, for Tuesday, ages ago. Th-there'll be other p-people . . ." And she burst out afresh. "O-o-oh! It's not f-*fair!*"

"Now, Robyn," said Jilly, "you've had your cry . . ."

But at that moment, there was a sort of rumbling sound from behind them. Michael spun round.

"Wh-what was that?" Robyn hiccoughed.

Michael, taking a careful step toward the stove, didn't answer.

"Just thunder, was it?" asked Jilly, looking up. "Were there storms predicted?"

"Oh, Jilly," said Robyn, "d'you really think he might get better in time?"

"Well . . ." Jilly began.

But the noise, a distant rumble not unlike thunder, sounded again. "That's funny," she said, instead, and turned, casually, just in time to catch the sugar bowl.

"What the—?"

The kitchen went wild. Plates, glasses, bottles, cutlery, and knickknacks flew across the room, smashed against the walls. The taps were suddenly flooding at full pelt,

153

the light was switching itself on and off, and the fridge door was opening and shutting, releasing gusts of chilly air.

"Out!" roared Michael, shoving them into the hallway, ducking to avoid a flying plate—and they huddled against the wall, peeping gingerly through the door.

Jilly yelled, *"What is it?"*

Michael yelled, "Keep your head down!"

And Robyn just wailed.

The pandemonium continued as they cowered there, clutching one another, helpless. But it was like popping corn—there was only so much corn to pop. And after a while the smashing and crashing grew less, and the noise subsided. The last thing to go was their grandmother's plant, from the windowsill. After that, a strange stillness, punctuated only by Robyn's snuffles, settled on the house.

They allowed a decent interval to elapse. Then, cautiously, they picked their way into the room through the broken china.

"I don't believe it!" said Jilly. She sank onto a chair. "Whatever will *Gran* say?"

Michael sighed. "That," he said, "is the least of our worries."

For a moment, there was a shaken silence. Then Jilly said tensely: "And what exactly do you mean by that?"

Michael gazed at her, tiredly. "Oh, look," he said, "you're not going to play dumb, are you?"

"I don't know what you're talking about—"

"Jilly, you've *seen* it. What the hell d'you think has happened?"

"Don't you swear at me. There's no need to—"

"Michael," said Robyn, in a small voice. "It could've been an earth tremor, couldn't it?"

Michael shrugged and waded over to the broom cupboard. "Whatever you say, Robyn. Just make up a nice story and believe in it. Don't face up to anything nasty, whatever you do. That's the way to get on around here . . ."

At that point, Juliet burst into tears. Michael groaned in annoyance, slammed the cupboard door, and looked up to see Simon standing in the doorway.

"*Hell!*" said Simon. Michael gazed mutely across the kitchen. Robyn began to gabble something about earthquakes, then petered out into half-baked sniffles. But Jilly, wiping hurriedly at her eyes, did something totally out of character.

She said, "I hardly think it's any of your business."

Michael had never seen Simon taken aback. It was not a pleasant experience.

"I—I am sorry," he faltered, still standing in the doorway, as if he didn't know what else to do. "It's just—your Gran—I heard—er—noises—"

Jilly, staring at the floor, blushed crimson. Simon made a sort of gesture with his hand, then let it fall. And left the room.

Michael, pale, began to clean up.

They were winning.

A Question of Identity

It was a wild night, that one.

Michael, standing at the living-room window, twitched the curtains apart and stared out. The glass panes were rattling spasmodically, as if in the grip of a rhythmic sort of pain. Outside, clumps of wet leaves scuttled past the streetlights, and sheets of rain splatted over the roof. Michael felt cold in his stomach.

Robyn, lying in the next room, wheezing over a vaporizer, was singing. She always sang after an asthma attack, in a sweet and tuneless sort of way—and it sounded odd tonight, harmonizing with the husky alto of the wind. Michael sighed, let the curtain fall, and went into Robyn's room. Juliet, sitting on the bed with her hand palm down on Robyn's back, looked up. It was past twelve.

"You go to bed," she said softly, as Robyn's voice began to fade. "She's much better. She'll be asleep in a minute."

"That's all right," said Michael. "You sleep. I'll stay with her for an hour or so.

Jilly hesitated. "Well, that would be marvelous," she said gratefully. "I have to study tomorrow, and I'll never do it if I don't get some sleep. And if you were here, you could wake me up if she needed anything. You would, wouldn't you, Michael?"

"No risk of me playing nursie," said Michael dryly. "I'll get myself some blankets. Could you get a pillow?"

Five minutes later, Michael was lying in a nest of rugs on the carpet in Robyn's darkened, steamed-up bedroom, watching the shadows writhe on the wall. Light from a streetlamp, streaming through the latticed window, projected a magnified pair of crosses just above his head, and branches, smudged masses, wagged through them fitfully. The shadows of the leaves were like moving stains. Michael gazed into them and thought: We're losing.

What got to him most was his being on the outside. He was powerless; he could only help when someone crossed his path. And if nothing from the War ever crossed his path again, there would be nothing at all he could do about it. It was funny, in a way. Even if they had won, he wouldn't have understood it. And now they were losing, as he felt in his bones they were, he understood it even less.

Robyn, a dim, lumpy shape on her bed, stirred and sighed wheezily. Michael wriggled, then sat up in agitation. Hugging the pillow, he peered fixedly at the wall.

Dancing in the shadows was a small, circular patch of light, the sort of spot you'd get from a flashlight—only different, somehow. Michael got up carefully and went over to the window. But there was nothing outside—nothing to give off a light like that. Michael watched his shadow, now mixing with the others on the wall, and impulsively stepped across the window, to block out the light from the street. But the bright patch remained, dancing in the center of Michael's shadow. It had an existence of its own.

"What are you?" he whispered.

For a moment it just sat there, glowing out at him. Then, suddenly, it began to trace his shadow. Around the head, down one arm, along the side and around the legs, up the other side, and back to the middle. It was like a salute, and Michael almost laughed.

"Are you in the War?" he whispered.

It paused and then moved rapidly up and down, as if nodding.

"Do—do you know how we're going?" asked Michael, then thought, he can only say yes or no. So he amended: "Are—are we winning?"

But the little spot only flicked from side to side, as if shaking its head.

Michael's heart sank. He said huskily, "Isn't there any hope at all?"

The question seemed to hang, solid, above them. The spot was still for a moment. Then, suddenly, it went for another tour around Michael's shadow.

Michael smiled, confusedly. "I—I don't understand," he whispered. "I—"

But the wind, howling about the window, interrupted him. The shadows writhed, and the little spot seemed to waver.

"What is it?" Michael hissed, alarmed.

For it was leaving his shadow, as if being dragged. Michael stood for a moment, dismayed, and then darted over toward it. But it was too late. The shadows, wagging with the wind, seemed to engulf it. Michael stumbled over to the wall, scrabbled uselessly at it with his hands.

But the shadows, though they flickered on his body, could not be touched.

———

The room was too dark, after that. Michael, in desperation, wondered when the night would end. And he could think of only one thing to do. He had to go back to the beginning.

For Michael was still the Devine family's resident insomniac. So he went out to the kitchen, and began to make a cheese sandwich. He made no noise.

He went into the darkened living room, stared at the space where the budgie's cage used to be, and devoured bread and cheese mechanically. When he went back to the kitchen, there was someone tapping on the window.

The Sparrow crawled in carefully over the sink, with one arm still limp by his side. His dark suit and fair hair were soaked with rain, and he had his collar turned up.

"I'm sorry, Devine," he gasped, ducking away from the window. "Did I frighten you?"

Michael smiled slightly. "You always say that. Can I get you anything?"

"No, thank you," said the Sparrow. "There's nothing more you can do."

He ducked his head and briefly raised his gray eyes to Michael's face. Then he looked away.

"I—I don't understand . . ." said Michael. "We beat them in so many things. We were winning."

The Sparrow tightened his lips, raised his shoulders in a slight shrug.

"The parts are ready, you might say, Devine. That's true. But the parts are meaningless unless they're joined together to make a whole. Meaningless—and weak. It's my job to assemble them. To make that strong whole. But I am failing. They have weakened me, and I am weakening more every minute. They are breaking through our defenses. Soon They will begin to undo what we have done . . . and the mission will be lost."

"Soon . . . ?"

"When they have destroyed me."

Michael stared at him. His eyes felt hot and prickling.

"Don't look like that, Devine." The Sparrow spoke sharply. "This battle may be lost, but the War will go on." His voice dropped, until he was nearly whispering. Michael strained to catch his words.

"For me—and those depending on me . . ." said the Sparrow, "it is nearly over. But there are many others to take up the banner."

Michael winced. "But—but—"

"I never promised you victory, Devine. I simply asked you to help. It's not your fault—you did your job."

"But what about Them?"

"Don't worry, you won't have any more trouble. You're small fry, Devine—as long as you can't help, you don't mean a thing to Them. Anyway," he added, without emotion, "They're after me now. I'm going to the Other Side. The fight will end there, one way or another."

"But you said—next time . . ."

"Just be quiet now and listen. I want you to go downstairs and keep watch by that mirror until dawn. So long as you are watching, nothing can come in. And if you do that for a night, it will be finished for you. Devine, are you listening?"

Michael looked up stubbornly.

"There must be some way I can help—I want to so

much. Always that's helped, before. Just that. The Swan-ningwren, the Gray Man, they . . ."

The Sparrow smiled ruefully. "The time has passed for that, Devine. Now, listen to me. You are a *Helper*; you are under my command. I have never had to remind you, before. Now do as I say. Please."

Michael bit his lip. The Sparrow held out his hand, and Michael took it.

"Well, good-bye," said the Sparrow. And, with a flutter and sigh, he was gone.

Michael walked slowly out of the kitchen. The War, like a merry-go-round on which creatures and people and events rode up and down and round and round, was spinning before him in a huge, giddy circle. As he glanced into Robyn's bedroom, the Swanningwren came round—unreal, but warm in his pajama shirt—then, Selby Lane, and the girl, beckoning, whispering. Michael rubbed his eyes, and went slowly down the first flight of stairs.

That place, and that—woman. And the Lady Deirdre, standing like a white swan by the shore. Michael, passing Simon's door, saw again that other Principal, and won-dered how far They would have gone. But then, he wasn't worth it, now. He was—what was it? —"small fry." Well, he thought, as the Gray Man rode past him—at least people would stop thinking he was mad now.

Michael, pausing in the laundry, saw the brown robe and the angular smile of the young man in the church. *He* had seemed pretty confident. Perhaps there was a chance, despite what the Sparrow had said. The little spot had seemed to think so. But then, thought Michael morosely, look what happened to *him*.

He went slowly into his room, shut the door and contemplated defeat. He grimaced as he remembered Sarah Jane. He couldn't possibly call her at this hour. Still, she was safe, at least, and so was he now.

But he knew, as he pulled down the bedclothes, that he would do it all again, without hesitating, despite the danger. Things like the hill in the moonlight—oh, it had all been worth it, a thousand times over. And now—now, it was finished.

Michael sat on the edge of the bed. *SEI*, he thought. The password, the universal greeting in the Secret War. *Sympathy, empathy, i* . . . He sat upright. A war across time, place—and even identity, the Sparrow had said. *Identity*, thought Michael.

For *SEI* was a formula, wasn't it? They'd had sympathy. They'd had empathy. But the last initial—well, it hadn't been used up, yet, had it? And if it really stood for identity—which surely it must—could that be a way of . . . ?

Michael stared deep into the cracked mirror. The Sparrow had been weakened. They were breaking through, he'd said. The Mission was failing—and the Sparrow was in grave danger. But if, after all, there was some way that Michael could help . . . ?

All the same, even if it was identity—what did it mean, in the Secret War? He had never had to work out how to help before. It had been automatic, provided for him. And identity, on its own, didn't seem to make much sense.

But then, there was Robyn. And—and *melting*. She had seemed a different person, in that dress—there had to be a clue, there, somewhere. *SEI*, thought Michael. Well, he understood the first two. Sympathy was feeling for someone in trouble, and empathy meant putting yourself in someone else's place. But identity—that didn't fit, surely. It meant . . . but still, maybe it had a couple of meanings. The dictionary!

There was a *Pocket Oxford* on his desk. Michael stumbled over to it, flicked through F, G, H—*Iceland, ideal, identical . . .*

Iděn'titў, n. Absolute sameness . . .

Michael shut the dictionary, came slowly back to the mirror. The crack cut his reflection in two. He stared at it. He had been walking a tightrope, his arms outstretched, teetering between two worlds. The crack had divided his reality. Could it also divide his self?

Michael sat up. "All right," he said suddenly, into the mirror. "I let *you* in. Now you let *me* in . . ."

And just before he felt himself get up and pass on through the crack, he thought he saw the reflection of another person where his own had been. The face was the Sparrow's.

SEI
Is Accomplished

In the darkened room, the woman waited, clutching the lacy edge of her pink-satin negligée.

There was a stealthy tread in the hall; the door opened . . .

"Oh, it's you, Laura. Why don't you turn on the light?

The woman looked at him under her eyelashes and smiled, ever so slightly. Then, from the breast of her negligée, drew a revolver . . .

"Shouldn't you be in bed, love?"

Sarah Jane, sitting small on the living room floor, wrapped in a blanket, her eyes glued to the television, started. Her father stood yawning in the doorway.

"But it's a storm," she said.

"So what d'you want me to do—sing 'A Few of My Favorite Things' for you? Come on, up you get."

Sarah Jane sighed, sorted arms from legs and dragged herself to her feet. She left a lingering look toward Laura (who, with the gun trembling in her outstretched hands, was just about to . . .), gathered up the blanket and yawned up the stairs.

But could not sleep.

The storm, moaning around her room, was like the Big Bad Wolf: *I'll huff, and I'll puff, and I'll*—Sarah Jane sat up in the darkness, hugging her knees. What she hated about storms was the thought of the things that were caught outside. Like the birds that would be dead in the morning and the little, whimpering things that seemed to scratch at the window. And storms reminded her of all the horrible parts in stories. Like that bit with the hand, in *Wuthering Heights*. And poor Oliver's mother, in the movie, about to have a baby in the rain at the front gate of the workhouse . . .

Sarah began to suck her thumb. It wasn't difficult to believe in the War, and things lurking, on a night like this. The rain rattled on against the windowpane, and Sarah Jane worried about the Sparrow.

A vision of Laura holding the revolver against her breast suddenly visited her. It had been all right while she was watching it, but now it seemed inexplicably sinister. Suddenly she felt rather sick. She got up, switched on the bedside lamp, flicked on the radio, and wandered a little around the room. Then she caught a glimpse of herself in the mirror and went over to get a better look.

"It's coming up to half-past one on a Sunday morning—still raging, are we?—and believe it or not we can look forward to a mild day with sunny periods, with a high of nineteen degrees Celsius. Here's a newie from The Smash . . ." Tinny music filled the room.

It was always horrible to look at yourself in the middle of the night when you couldn't sleep. Sarah Jane shuddered, then, suddenly, thought of the crack in that other mirror—and Michael.

There was, abruptly, a nagging, empty feeling of fear in her stomach. She had a horrible conviction that Michael had done something reckless. For he was reckless, she knew. He wasn't very brave, but he was reckless. If the opportunity should present itself . . .

She crept into bed and sank back onto the pillow. Slowly, her thoughts merged into nightmares.

When she awoke, the radio was playing "Penny Lane," and the clock said 4:07. It was still raining. Sarah Jane had a headache. She was also absolutely certain of something: Michael was in trouble.

Sarah Jane got up, stared out the window, and thought. Calling was out of the question—the phone was in her father's bedroom, and besides, it would mean waking the whole family. She could call Simon, she supposed—but even as she contemplated it she knew that calling wasn't enough. She had, somehow, to get to Michael in person. Sarah Jane began to pull on clothes. If she couldn't use the phone, she couldn't call a taxi, either. She would have to get a bus. But she didn't even know if there were any buses at that time of the morning.

Sarah Jane stopped and thought. All the warnings she had ever heard about going out by yourself in the middle of the night were whirling round and round in her head. But somehow, all the warnings counted for nothing against the horrible fact of the War itself. Normally, it would've been an idiotic thing to do, but now . . .

She switched off the radio, and the light, then she shut the bedroom door, crept along the hall past her father snoring solitary in the double bed, and slipped gingerly down the stairs. She knew the last one creaked, so she missed it. Very slowly, she opened the door.

The rain, coming in gusts, whipped through the door and struck her in the face. She had forgotten to bring an umbrella, but wasn't about to go back now. So she shut the door, pulled her coat around her, buried her hands in her pockets—and turned her nose toward Coleridge.

It was very dark, and after a while she realized that she must have passed the bus stop without seeing it. What an idiot! Still, if she walked along far enough, she would eventually come across another one. Then she could look at the timetable, and if a bus wasn't coming in the near future, she would walk to the next one, and so on. Sarah Jane had never caught a bus to Coleridge before, but she didn't really care. She would go mad if she couldn't keep moving.

So she walked, and walked—and walked.

She was very wet, now. Her hair fell lank and matted down her black-duffle back, and her legs began to itch with the damp inside her jeans. The sky was purple and undulating; the clouds swelled and traveled like monstrous beings, and the street was beginning to look unfamiliar.

Sarah Jane tried to remember exactly where Coleridge was. She turned right tentatively at the next corner and suddenly saw a bus stop.

She forgot everything and ran toward it. Breathing hard, she scanned the timetable. Twice. But Coleridge wasn't even mentioned.

In a minute, thought Sarah Jane. I'll find out where I am. I must have got a bit muddled, that's all. There *is* a Coleridge bus stop somewhere around here. I'll just go back a little way and take the other turning. But for now . . .

She sat down on the curb and cried. And the Sparrow, sitting next to her in the wet, politely offered her a handkerchief.

"Pull yourself together, Yardley. I have a job for you."

Sarah Jane gasped. The Sparrow, his hair flattened by the rain so that his very pointed ears showed clearly, looked worn and dogged and curiously gentle.

"Don't worry; it's going to be all right. However, we must hurry."

"But—but Michael . . ."

"He has been in danger, and it is important that you should be with him. I am no use. He needs one of his own to call him back. To call him—Yardley, are you listening?"

"I—I—"

"Just tell him, *SEI* is accomplished."

"S-*SEI* is accomp—"

"Right." The Sparrow peered through the rain at the green thing on his wrist. "I must go. There is much to be done. But I think I can solve your transport problems."

———

Juliet awoke in the bleak dawn with a vague burden of worry. There was something, she felt sure—oh, that's right. Gran was away, wasn't she? And Auntie Alice was sick. So she sat up, rubbed her eyes—and knew that that wasn't it. Well, what was it, then? Oh, of course—Robyn. Jilly climbed downstairs.

But Robyn was already up, sitting on the table in the kitchen, with her legs swinging. As Jilly came in, she looked up, sat still, and looked at her with a strained expression.

"Jilly," she said huskily. "I'm scared."

Jilly switched on the light. "No wonder," she said, "sitting here all alone in the dark. Why didn't you come and wake me up?"

Robyn looked away; began to swing her legs again.

"D'you think—d'you think things might start flying again, Jilly?"

Jilly glanced around nervously. That was one question for which she could not find a comfortable reply. "I—I don't think so, Rob."

Robyn swung her legs. "Where's Michael?" she said.

"Downstairs, I guess."

But Robyn wasn't listening.

"Jilly," she said, "there's someone knocking."

Juliet paused. "You've got good ears," she said, after a moment. "So there is."

They looked nervously at each other.

"Wh-who could it be?" said Robyn.

"Maybe we shouldn't answer it," said Jilly slowly. "At this hour of the morning . . . ."

But the knocking continued, faintly, from downstairs.

"Trouble is," said Jilly, "it could be something urgent." And then: "Oh, come on."

They went downstairs.

At first, Jilly hardly recognized her. She was standing, pale, on the doorstep, sopping wet and straggly, looking as if she wasn't quite sure where she was. When the door opened, she said rather blindly:

"I have to see Michael."

Jilly almost screamed.

But, with Robyn and Sarah Jane hovering behind, she did manage to get downstairs.

———

Simon Collins was roused from his work by a tentative knock on the door. His first thought was Michael, and he wondered, as he wiped the first layer of paint from his hands, if anything had gone wrong.

But when he opened the door, he was more than a little taken aback to discover the Sleeping Beauty—pale in her light-green bathrobe, with her neat wings of wavy fair hair sitting primly on her shoulders.

"Juliet . . ."

"I'm terribly sorry, Simon, b-but I'm worried about Michael."

"Michael?" said Simon. He went as if to put his hand on her arm, then changed his mind.

"He—he's just—*sitting* there . . ."

"What, in his room? D'you want me to come down?"

"P-please . . ."

Jilly put her fist to her mouth. Simon frowned at her. Then said: "Well, come on."

He led her downstairs.

In the cellar room, Michael sat motionless, staring into the mirror. Sarah Jane, with her mass of dark hair tangled down her back, stood as if frozen, with her hand on the dressing table. And Robyn, pressed to the doorway, looked on, confused and frightened. The electric light, shining down on them, made them all seem paler than they really were, and outside, rain dripped through the garden. The only sound was the gurgle of the drainpipes.

Sarah Jane looked around at them wordlessly. Whatever she had been expecting to find in Michael's room, it wasn't this. The thing on the bed was only a shell. How could she talk to it?

Simon glanced worriedly at her.

"Michael?" he said.

But Michael, very still, stared on into the mirror.

170

Simon bit his lip. "Come on, Mike," he said. "What's up?"

The rain dripped in the drainpipes; Robyn began to wheeze. Michael, silent and stiff, stared into the mirror. Simon moved in closer; frowned into his face. Then he hesitated and laid a hand quite suddenly on Michael's forehead.

"He's cold as ice!" he exclaimed. Jilly dragged a blanket off the bed. Simon took Michael's hand and began to rub rapidly up and down his arm. Then looked up at Sarah, who still stood palely by the mirror.

"Isn't there anything . . .? I mean, don't you know . . .?

Jilly, trying to settle the blanket around Michael, looked up oddly.

Sarah Jane looked at Simon. "I—I—"

"You *must* know something." Then, seeing that she was frightened, he added firmly, "Just come over and talk to him."

Jilly said nervously: "Don't you think we ought to be getting a doctor?"

"A witch doctor, maybe," Simon said dryly.

And the figure on the bed looked up at Sarah Jane unseeingly. The dry lips opened. A harsh rasping began, deep in the throat. Words struggling to form.

"Lost . . . no way . . . back . . . no . . . me . . ."

An electric current ran through the room. Sarah Jane felt it shock her and suddenly knew what she had to do. If she said the Sparrow's words to the shell, perhaps it would be Michael again. She leaned over, took a deep breath, and said, very firmly indeed:

"Michael—*SEI* is accomplished."

For one ghastly moment, he seemed to be fading.

Then, another Michael stepped back out of the mirror and merged with the figure on the bed. He blinked, stretched, yawned, and looked up to find them arranged like statues around his room.

"It's all right," he said, as if to young children. "We've won."

The Mirror Heals

Juliet, thought Michael in the car on Tuesday night, had finally woken up. Graceful in her best dress, which was soft and smoky gray and sort of flowing, she said to Sarah Jane: "So you weren't even missed?"

Sarah, picking up the half-smothered disapproval in her voice, said defensively: "Well, what he doesn't know won't hurt him. And after all, Jilly, you can't really worry about parents when you've got magic on your hands."

"Out, damned spot!" said Simon, being Lady Macbeth. "You washed them thoroughly, I hope?"

They giggled appreciatively. Simon, finding a parking spot, maneuvered himself into it, and turned off the ignition. They slid out of the car, and Simon locked the doors.

The parking lot, a makeshift affair in the backyard of the Railway Institute, was grassy and only dimly lit by the lights from the hall itself. They waded carefully around other people's cars, Sarah Jane and Juliet walking ahead slightly. Next to Simon, Michael thrust his hands in his pockets, and sighed. Simon hesitated, then said abruptly:

"Well—what d'you make of it, Michael?"

Michael paused, staring ahead. He was thinking about

the last two weeks. About the letters on the sand, and the crack in the mirror, and the Sparrow. About the Swanningwren, and the room that wasn't there, and the Lady Deirdre. About those creatures, those evil creatures in the alley. About that man in the hospital. And about the final step he had taken. The step that had almost destroyed him. Such a variety, Michael thought, and yet all, somehow, part of the same process.

What *did* he make of it, the Secret War?

"You know," he began at last, "sometimes, in World War Two, when they were constructing something top secret, they'd get hundreds of people working separately on different parts, and each person would only ever see the one component he or she was in charge of. I read it somewhere. It was incredible. I mean, there'd be this bloke, for instance, making all these little round metal things with the letter 'Z' on them, and he wouldn't even have the slightest idea what sort of machine they were going into. But, you see, he'd know that in the end whatever it was would help win the war. So he'd just keep on making his little round thing with the letter 'Z' on it . . ."

"Until the war was won?" Simon suggested.

"Yes," said Michael. "Well, I reckon that's what the Secret War is like. People—and creatures"—(and even saints from church windows, he thought)—"all playing their part in a mission, without ever knowing exactly what that mission was. Sometimes the things they were doing didn't make much sense—not on their own. But the mission—the whole machine with all the components put together—that was all that really mattered. All of them were helping, in their different ways. And me and Sarah Jane—I guess *we* were helping by helping *them . . .*"

Simon looked at him.

"I think I begin to follow you," he said.

"Maybe," said Michael, "maybe it's not all that hard to understand, after all. The Secret War—the Secret War is just the battle between good and evil. It's going on everywhere, all the time. It's so—so constant, and so basic, that everything you do, every word you say, every decision you make—is fighting either on one side or the other. Everyone's in it—the Secret War. It's just that, me and Sarah Jane—we got to fight it in a special way . . ."

Simon was silent. Jilly, under the entrance light, fished tickets out of her handbag. The hall, warm and three-quarters full, hummed welcome.

"Oh good," said Michael, seeing plenty of nice, inconspicuous seats. "We can sit down the back, can't we?"

Not as far as a small, spruced-up usherette was concerned. She pounced on them and led the way to four seats in the third row.

Michael glanced nervously at the stage; much too close for comfort.

"We *can't* sit here," he hissed. "She might even see us."

"Oh," said Jilly. "She wouldn't like that."

Clairvoyant Simon had never actually sat down. "Come on," he said, ushering them back into the aisle. "All we have to do is avoid that kid . . ."

They made a furtive escape and managed to settle unobtrusively just behind the main throng of people. Then they played musical chairs for the obligatory few seconds, and Juliet found herself unexpectedly next to Simon.

"Oh, wouldn't you rather be near Michael?" she said ingenuously.

"No, don't bother," said Simon heroically. "I don't mind." He caught Michael's eye, and they both looked away hurriedly.

Sarah Jane waved at someone in the front row. "There's Lyn Brady," she said.

Simon glanced at his watch. "A miracle recovery, was it?" he said lightly. "I thought they'd called it off?"

"Well," said Jilly, "the Prince does seem all right. I saw him, this evening, when I walked Rob down. His nose is a bit blocked, though. I hope he doesn't have to blow it . . ."

"Shh!" said Michael, sitting up. "It's starting!"

———

Backstage, when it was all over, children shouted, smeared cold cream, peeled off stockings, and cried over missed lines. The ruffled rabble of the dressing room smelled of baby powder and cheap lipstick. Michael, coming down to collect Robyn, stood shyly in the doorway.

She spotted him first. Limping into a sock, she waved precariously, and so he slouched over to her, through half-changed princes and wizards and fairy godmothers. He wasn't looking, but no one seemed to mind very much, anyway. Robyn was in the middle of a group of five little girls. One, a developing Jilly, was folding up Robyn's costume.

"Hello, Michael," they all said.

"Hi," said Michael briefly. "I thought you were fantastic. All of you."

"Gee, thanks, did you really? Gosh, Michael." They

176

paused momentarily, impressed by such an ancient presence, then began to shout at him about what had gone wrong.

It was then that he began to understand.

For he was feeling it with them; he *was*. He knew what they were about, behind their flushed greasy faces. And yet, he had never been in their play—he was just audience, an outsider.

And it was this—his being perpetually on the fringe— that had gotten Michael into the Secret War. For it was obvious, he thought, as they gabbled on at him. If he had planted himself totally in one layer, he would not have had time to take on another. But in either world, Michael had only ever been a sort of visitor.

And that reminded him, somehow, of Identity. The Secret War had meant sacrifice. He had given his sympathy, then his empathy, and then, finally, the greatest thing he had—his identity. But how strange it was that identity had two meanings. *Absolute sameness*, the dictionary had told him, and yet, as he'd just been thinking, it also meant your personality, your self. It was like Robyn had said—you don't stop being yourself. You just start being someone else. It was only when you were most completely yourself—most certain of your own identity—that you could actually become another person; sacrifice that self of yours in order to suffer, not just through sympathy, or even empathy, but entirely *as one* with the sufferer.

The Sparrow had been the sufferer. Michael had suffered—not only *with* him—but *as* him. And *SEI* was accomplished. The battle was won.

Then, amid the romp and the rabble of the dressing room, there was someone behind him.

"Michael?" said the girl with the long dark hair. "Michael," said Sarah Jane, "come quickly. The Sparrow's here."

———

From the fence down the back of the Institute hall, you had quite a good view of the hill. But tonight there were no lights on the gentle slope, only those of the still-humming hall and the wavering glow of the Sparrow himself.

"I won't ask," said Michael. "Only—is everything really going to be all right?"

The Sparrow, leaning on the fence in his trim dark suit, said: "The mission is accomplished." And smiled.

The breeze bore faint voices from the hall. A car door slammed shut, light diminished, and crickets creaked.

"So . . . you're on leave, Devine," the Sparrow said formally.

"On *leave*? But what'll I do?"

"You could try resting up. Or you could write one of those adventure stories you seem to be so keen on."

"Oh, cripes," said Michael.

"Well, your older sister's an artist. And your younger sister's an actress. I may as well tell you."

"What?"

"Well, perhaps I shouldn't," said the Sparrow, "but you are going to be a writer, actually, Devine, whether you like it or not. So you may as well start now."

Michael, silent, stared out over the hill. Sarah Jane said: "What about me?"

The Sparrow ducked his head and peered up at her with gray eyes. It was a habit with him. He said: "Yardley, if I could put you on leave, I would. However, I don't think you need it, and I don't think you'd take it. But, please be careful. And next time, take your umbrella."

Sarah Jane grinned. The Sparrow lifted his injured arm and looked carefully at the green thing on his wrist. Then glanced up suddenly at Michael, who was standing very still, his head down.

"Oh, Devine," he said, with a flicker of concern. "You don't understand, do you?"

Michael swallowed. "Understand what?" he said.

The Sparrow smiled, pink and white. "Once you've seen the war, Devine, you're in it. Nothing can change that. You're on the merry-go-round. Just sit tight. It'll bring you back to me in its own time. Back to me—or someone like me." He stopped and again looked straight into Michael's eyes.

"How much do you remember?" he said.

Michael knew what he meant. "Not much," he said truthfully. "Just feelings—just a feeling, and—and gray, and a beating sound. And then suddenly knowing we'd won, and I was—outside—again. Will you . . .?"

"No," said the Sparrow quickly. "No, I can't. What you did was . . . extraordinary, Devine. At your level quite—well, almost—unprecedented. The danger was immense. It was a reckless, reckless act. You must never do it again. Do you hear me?"

Michael nodded, biting his lip. The Sparrow touched his shoulder, and he looked up.

"However," said the Sparrow, "it is thanks to your reck-lessness that I am here, and for that I thank you. For that we all thank you."

"Then—then—"

"I am asking you to do me a favor, Devine. Just lie low for a while. You're almost more than I can cope with."

For a moment, Michael hardly knew where to look.

179

The Sparrow continued: "I told you, you're on leave. So am I." He shrugged at his injured arm. "I have to get this fixed up, you know."

There was a short pause. Then, impulsive as he had been that night in the snow, the Sparrow laid a hand on Michael's shoulder and, for a moment, just looked at him. With anyone else, Michael would have had to lower his eyes; with the Sparrow it was different. Looking at him made Michael feel that everyone else was only half-alive.

"You have friends in both worlds, now, Devine," said the Sparrow.

He stood back, and with an expression faintly quizzical, shot each of them a last, quick glance. "*SEI*," he said.

And, with a flutter and a sigh, was gone.

———

Inside the shadowy doorway of No. 4, Jilly fumbled for the light.

"You right?" said Simon softly, over a sleeping Robyn.

"Yes, here it is," Jilly whispered, flicking the switch. The hallway flooded with light, and they all blinked. Robyn, stirring, said, "Jilly?"

"I'm here. Woken up, have you? Come on," she said, taking her hand as Simon let her down on the floor. "Come on, you're too heavy for *me*."

"I was good, wasn't I?"

"Marvelous."

"And I didn't miss a single line, did I?"

"Not one. Bed, Robyn."

"What about the bit where I—"

"That was good, too. Off with shoes . . ."

Jilly's voice faded into Robyn's pink and white

bedroom. Simon, gazing bluely after them, stood irresolute in the doorway.

"You'd better come in," said Michael.

"It's a bit late," said Simon.

Michael sighed and raised his voice. "Simon's going, Jilly," he called, loud and cruel.

Simon just looked at him. Juliet, coming out of Robyn's bedroom, shut the door quietly and said: "Won't you stay for coffee, Simon?"

"Oh—I—er—"

"I really don't mind. I'm making some, for us, anyway."

"Oh, all right, then."

Of course, thought Michael, he couldn't sound *pleased*. That wouldn't do at all. But when Jilly went into the kitchen, Simon winked at him.

"You coward," said Michael, scandalized.

"Pardon?" called Jilly from the kitchen.

"When d'you think your gran'll be back?" called Simon quickly.

Juliet came to the doorway. "Well," she said, "Auntie Alice's on the mend, you know. Or at least, that's what I gathered on the phone last night. Only she's had a fright, and so I think Gran feels obliged to stay on for a bit."

"In other words," said Michael to Simon, "not in the next forty-eight hours."

"I think I can manage without an interpreter, thank you," said Jilly tartly. "Simon, won't you go in and sit down? Michael can find the light."

Michael switched it on. Simon, still slightly uneasy, said: "Robyn *was* good, you know. I mean, really."

"Yes, I'm afraid you're right," said Jilly, coming in.

"You make it sound like a failing," said Michael.

"Oh, it's not that. It's just that—well, it's a pity she couldn't be good at something that wasn't such a heartbreak to get into."

"Well, she probably wouldn't fancy the post office," said Simon. "You're a talented family, you lot."

"If you mean my painting . . ." began Jilly derisively.

"I never did get to see any. I mean, I could probably help . . ." said Simon off-handedly.

"What, now?" said Jilly gently.

Simon suddenly looked prepared for anything. "Have you got any here?"

"They're all here," laughed Jilly. Then she hesitated, and said, "P'raps I should just pop upstairs and get some." She glanced at Simon and climbed lightly up to the attic.

Michael, for some reason, had to giggle for a moment.

"It's not funny," said Simon.

Michael composed himself. "No," he said. "Sorry."

But Simon only frowned at him. "D'you know," he said, "if it hadn't 've been for your War . . ."

Jilly reappeared. "They're pretty awful," she warned, as people do.

And Michael, watching as they bent over sheets of artpaper, suddenly remembered the faults he had seen in their paintings. It occurred to him that a painting with Simon's honesty and Jilly's kindness would not be such a bad effort . . .

"D'you really think so?"

"Yes, it's very real. You're timid with your colors, though, aren't you? I don't like that line, there . . ."

"It distorts it, I know. Only . . ."

"Well, look: a bit more of an angle. Like *that*."

"Oh, yes, I see! That's much better."

Michael was suddenly superfluous. Quietly he slipped downstairs.

———

The mirror gleamed like still water, smooth and unmarked. The crack had gone. There would be no more traffic spilling through the gap. The room was just as it had been before the War slithered into it.

Michael sat, depressed, on the bed and wondered however he would explain *that* to his grandmother. His tired reflection, whole once more, offered no brilliant suggestions. It would tell him only that, whatever the Sparrow might say, the play was over.

But then . . .

On leave, was he? Michael looked more closely at his reflection. Somehow the Michael he saw there was a lot more Michael than he had ever been before. There was something in that, he supposed. And then, there was the Sparrow. The Sparrow, in his dark suit, with his competence and his tentative kindness. And that odd flutter and sigh that seemed to travel away with him. A strange, lovely sound. A beating; a breeze.

Almost, thought Michael idly, like—

Wings.